"You look great, David."

"Thanks." He grinned. "Have to say that freedom agrees with me. You look beautiful, Billie."

"I look sweaty and I smell like beer, but if that's your kind of gal..."

"You're my kind of girl."

I blushed.

Suddenly, C.C. screamed.

I looked up at the bar's television. The anchor said, "And in a shocking twist to the release of inmate David Falco, a woman was murdered tonight in Jersey City. Sources tell CNN that the crime included a playing card left on the body. The suicide king..."

Dear Reader,

Thank you so much for purchasing the first book of my new Billie Quinn series. I wanted to write this book to show a little of the real life of CSIs—unsung heroes who gather the evidence and analyze it in the lab. As in all my books, the heroine is surrounded by an eccentric "family"—a motley crew of misfits and unusual people who comprise her circle of friends. In this book, you'll meet Lewis LeBarge, head of the crime lab, who has a penchant for collecting brains and photos of blood spatter; Sister C.C., a nun with a passion for prison ministry; Mikey, Billie's brother and a ne'er-do-well—but a sweetheart anyway; and the rest of the colorful characters, such as Tommy Two Trees, an FBI agent and, like Lewis, a denizen of New Orleans.

Billie herself is brainy but street smart. Her brother and father are both involved in the mob, but she has chosen to play it mostly straight in her life. She's haunted by her mother's murder, which has only drawn her closer to the people she loves.

I hope you enjoy Billie and her friends as they fight to clear a man in prison for murder utilizing new DNA technology. Prepare for suspense and action...and enjoy!

Erica Orloff

Erica
Orloff

TRACE
of Innocence

Published by Silhouette Books

America's Publisher of Contemporary Romance

SILHOUETTE BOOKS

ISBN 0-373-51389-5

TRACE OF INNOCENCE

www.SilhouetteBombshell.com

Printed in U.S.A.

Books by Erica Orloff

Silhouette Bombshell

Urban Legend #8
Knockout #19
†*The Golden Girl* #58
*Trace of Innocence #75

†The It Girls
*A Billie Quinn Case

Red Dress Ink

Spanish Disco
Diary of a Blues Goddess
Mafia Chic
Divas Don't Fake It
Do They Wear High Heels in Heaven?

MIRA Books

The Roofer
Double Down (as Tess Hudson)

ERICA ORLOFF

is a native New Yorker who relocated to sunny south Florida after vowing to never again dig her car out of the snow. She loves playing poker—a Bombshell trait—and likes her martinis dry. Visit her Web site at www.ericaorloff.com.

To my sister, Stacey, for always reading my books and being one of my biggest supporters.

Chapter 1

Blood spatter was artfully arranged.

Photographs of crime-scene blood spatter, in stark black and white, were matted and framed, lining a long hallway with hardwood floors that squeaked as I walked.

I had stopped thinking of the photos as gruesome or even odd two years ago when I started working for Lewis LeBarge, my boss at New Jersey's State Crime Laboratory and collector of all things macabre. He told me once that it came with the territory. "Spend enough time around the dead," he had said to me, his New

Orleans accent giving him a certain Southern charm, "and eventually you come up with ways to mock the Grim Reaper—just to let him know he hasn't won…yet." Lewis regularly talked to The Reaper like an old friend, asking him just how or why a dead body met its maker.

"Lewis?" I called out from the hallway. I had let myself in the front door of his old duplex in Weehawken.

"Up here," he called out. "The office."

I climbed the stairs. There were just two small bedrooms on the second story. One was the master bedroom, and the other he used as a home office, complete with Internet links to our database in the lab.

I poked my head in. "Ready?"

"For you, darlin', always." He winked at me, his prematurely gray hair giving him a distinguished look, making him seem older than his forty years.

I spied a new photo on the wall. The blood puddle next to the gunshot victim looked like black syrup. "Has anyone ever suggested to you that perhaps the reason you never make it past the first date with a woman is your taste in art?"

"Now, Billie, I'm just waitin' for you to realize we're the ones meant to be together. And until then—" he mock-sighed "—I remain alone and desperately lonely in this cold Northern city."

"Don't give me that…your New Orleans gentleman charm is a magnet for women. I've seen them clustered around you like bees buzzing around a flower."

"I never hurt for first dates, but, as you so kindly pointed out, it's getting to date number two that's difficult."

I looked over at the aquarium tank on the shelf, which housed an enormous tarantula he had named "Ripper," after the serial killer he once wrote a thesis on. I'm not squeamish—you can't be, working in a forensics lab—but spiders give me the creeps. Especially hairy ones.

"Maybe you should try telling them you do something sane. Boring, even. Ever try saying you're an accountant? Working with numbers all day is certainly an improvement over saying you spent the day examining brain matter."

"Eventually, I'd be found out. And with the exception of you, there aren't many women who enjoy discussin' blowflies on dead bodies and the rate of maggot infestation over a lovely supper of jambalaya."

"Really? I would have thought some women would love to hear all about it. Especially while eating." I rolled my eyes. "I've got you figured out. You, dear Lewis, love to scare them off."

"Perhaps I do." He winked at me. "How's that cop you've been dating?"

"Good…when he's on the wagon."

"And when he's not?"

"Come on, Lewis, neither of us has a stellar track record in the love department."

"We're both married to the job."

"I suppose we are. You ready?"

"Darlin', I wouldn't miss this chance to mingle with the underworld of New Jersey for anything. Your family is like an anthropological field study."

"Shut up," I snapped, but grinned at him as he stood up, ducking his head slightly to avoid hitting the overhead lamp. Lewis stood a lanky six foot two inches in his custom cowboy boots. He wore his standard-issue black Levi's and white oxford cloth shirt, well-worn at the elbows, with a pair of black onyx cuff links I swear he put on every shirt he wore. He turned off the lamp and the two of us made our way downstairs and out the door. My big maroon Cadillac was parked on the street.

"Still driving the Sherman land tank, I see."

"I can't part with it—despite how much gas

this thing guzzles. My uncle Sean left it to me when he went inside."

"'Inside,'" Lewis mused, as he climbed in the car Uncle Sean gave me when he drew thirty years for aggravated assault and murder—he'd not only killed his victim, but taken a hacksaw to him. "I do love how the Quinn family has such special euphemisms—like this party we're going to."

"What? It's a Welcome Home party for my father. What's wrong with that?"

"You mean a Welcome Home from *Rahway Prison* party. But no doubt your aunt Helen will make one of her wonderful cheesecakes for the occasion. I'm fond of the strawberry one. Very moist."

"Lewis, it's still a coming-home party, no matter where he was prior to actually coming home. Besides, this time was really stupid. A parole violation…busted at an illegal card game. I mean, come off it. You sometimes sit in with them, too."

I started the car and pulled away from the curb, biting my lip in irritation for a minute. There was nothing I hated more than cops going after bullshit crimes when murderers and child molesters were a plague.

Lewis leaned back against the plush velour

seats. "Well, all I can say is family parties with y'all is like stepping into a Scorsese film. I love bein' around your relatives. They are quite entertainin'."

I drove from Lewis's place to JFK Boulevard and eventually steered my way toward Hoboken, coping with heavy traffic.

"But you know, Billie, I've still never understood how it is you managed to turn out...honest and law-abiding, if a little unusual around the edges."

I shrugged, staring ahead at the highway. "I don't know."

"Come on, I know you've thought about it. You must have some explanation."

I had thought about it. Endlessly. Until my head hurt, sometimes. My mother had disappeared when I was nine. The cops had bungled the case, more interested in focusing on my father—head of an Irish crime family—than in uncovering the truth. When her body turned up six months later—nothing left but bones and the shreds of her dress—they arrested the wrong man, eventually freeing him without the case going to trial when his alibi was airtight. He'd been sitting in county lockup the night of her murder, on a DUI charge.

"I don't know, Lewis, I just wanted to solve

murders. And if I became a cop, my family would have disowned me. So working for you is about as close as I can get to fighting the bad guys legally. Why did you go into forensics?"

"You know. An obsession with blood and guts. Liked to drive my mama mad with bringin' home dead animals."

Of course, I knew Lewis's reasons ran as deep as my own. He'd been at Tufts, bent on an academic career as a scientist and college professor when the bayous of Louisiana began giving up their dead. One by one, floaters came to the surface, women tortured and murdered by a serial killer. One of the dead was his childhood sweetheart. His path changed, and he never looked back.

The two of us drove through the streets of Hoboken to Quinn's Pub, owned by my father's brother, Tony. If "pub" conjures up images of darts and leather booths, that's not Quinn's. It's a rough bar you don't go to unless you know Tony—or can hold your own among the tough guys who hang there after long shifts driving cement mixers, or otherwise breaking their backs earning a living. It's one of the last neighborhood places around. I parked the car around the corner on the street and the two of us made our way to the entrance. The sidewalks were already teeming with relatives and pals of my dad.

"Billie!" Tony threw his rock-hard, tattooed arms around me as we maneuvered our way inside, squeezing past the crowds. "Your dad's at the tables. How you doin', Lewis?"

"Fine, just fine," Lewis said, smiling and taking a bottle of beer offered to him by Pammie, a waitress in skin-tight black jeans and a Quinn's Pub T-shirt—black with a green shamrock embroidered on the chest. I saw her eye him flirtatiously.

I took Lewis's other hand so I wouldn't lose him as we snaked our way through the bar. We reached the back room, with its four pool tables. Dad was about to sink his last ball into the corner pocket. He let out a whoop when it went in, the ball spinning fast, and collected his forty bucks from his opponent. Then he spotted me and came over and planted a kiss on the top of my head.

"Billie." He smiled and looked at me, then grabbed me in a hug. With Dad and me, we don't have to say much. We know how we feel.

Dad stands about six feet tall—a good four inches taller than I am. We both have black hair, though his is now flecked with gray at the temples. We both have greenish-blue eyes. He has an olive complexion, though, and mine is pale with a smattering of freckles on my cheeks and nose. My nose turns up just a bit—and I look like a tomboy, with two deep dimples. Even though I'm twenty-nine, I still get carded when I buy beer at the grocery store.

"Good to see you, Daddy. Sorry I didn't get you from prison today—I was knee-deep in analyzing a shipment of drugs found in someone's trunk. Heroin. Street value near a million dollars. Uncle Tony said it wasn't a problem to go get you."

"Nah, not at all." Dad shook his head in disgust. "Besides, it's good to get that crap off the streets." The Quinn family had its hand in bookmaking, a little loan-sharking and trafficking in stolen property—mostly pirated DVDs. Occasionally, a Quinn family member will fight violence with violence. But my father won't tolerate drugs. Not just in my brother and me growing up, but in anyone who's going to have anything to do with the Quinn family.

"Want to play a game, Lewis? A friendly wager?"

Lewis looked at me and grinned. My father had to serve a four-month sentence for parole violation. The entire time, Lewis had been practicing his pool game. He was hoping to actually beat my father, something he hadn't been able to do since the day they met.

"As you so eloquently say, rack 'em up."

The two of them bet twenty bucks each, which I held in my right front pocket to make it official, and soon they were playing hot and heavy.

Despite Lewis's near-daily practice, he was still down two when we heard a commotion out front. Shouts rose above the usual din of the crowded pub, and I turned my head to see the crowd actually morphing, moving as it accommodated a growing brawl. A crowd in a bar fight seems to become a living thing.

"Christ, it's Murphy's boys," my father said.

Lewis looked at me quizzically.

"Hand me that," I said, gesturing to his pool cue. He did and I stood waiting. So did my father.

Within two minutes, the brawl had pushed its way into the pool room. I recognized three of my cousins and all five Murphy brothers going at it. One cousin connected with a solid left hook on the square chin of Pat Murphy, and let loose with a stream of expletives, ending with, "…that's what you get for beating up a woman."

That was enough for my father and me. I

hoisted the pool cue and brought it down on the shoulder of Jimmy "Tank" Murphy. He turned to take a swing at me, but I held the cue like a bat and gave him a solid swing right in the ribs. He fell back against a pool table, grabbed a glass and threw it at my face. It missed and shattered to the floor. Next thing I knew, a striped pool ball barely missed my forehead. Chairs were overturned, more glasses broke, and I decided I'd had enough.

I looked around at the escalating fight and knew Tank was the key to it. Whenever the biggest, burliest, nastiest Murphy went down, the other brothers usually fell in line. Blood poured from Tank's nose, but still he charged like a bull. I took the pool cue as he came at me and instead of swinging at his ribs, I lowered the cue and brought it up, with all my might, between his legs. He immediately collapsed as I connected with my intended pair of targets.

Slowly, surely, the brawl died down from there. The Murphy brothers were bounced out the door by Tony's three sons—one a muscle-bound bodybuilder the width of my Cadillac. The pub was a mess, but it was no showplace to begin with.

Lewis surveyed the wreckage. "Do y'all know how to throw a party without it ending up like the O.K. Corral?"

"It's an old feud."

"Feud? I'd say it's World War III."

"Come on." I kissed my father goodbye and gingerly climbed over the broken glass and chairs, making my way with Lewis outside. When we got out on the sidewalk and started walking to our car, I said, "My brother, Mikey, fell in love with the youngest Murphy sister. They've been living together for a year now."

"Isn't your brother in prison at the moment?"

"Yeah. He gets out next month. But Marybeth and my brother are still sickeningly in love. Anyway, there's bad blood with the Murphys. Always has been. My father and old man Murphy used to fight it out over bookmaking territory. And the brothers are really not nice guys. I take it one of them hit a girl tonight. But really, it's old stuff—mostly having to do with Dad."

"Your father was involved in illegal activity?" Lewis asked with mock horror.

I punched him in the arm. "Go back to the South, you ass."

"So these Murphys, they just show up and start brawls?"

"Pretty much."

"You're quite handy with that pool cue."

"Practice. My father and brother have been

hustling pool my whole life. Sometimes people don't take too kindly to losing."

"I was so close to beating him tonight."

"No, you weren't."

"But I was!"

"Lewis, you've improved, but Minnesota Fats doesn't have to worry."

We turned a corner, and I immediately stopped in my tracks and put my arm out to halt Lewis, too.

"Wish I'd brought that pool cue," I muttered. Because there, sitting on the hood of my land tank, was the biggest, most hulking man I'd ever seen in my life. And he was clearly waiting for us.

Chapter 2

"Can I help you?" I asked warily.

The man slid off my hood and stood on the sidewalk, thrusting out his hand, which was the size of a baseball mitt. "Joe Franklin," he said, smiling.

I didn't take his hand. "What do you want?"

"A minute of both of your time."

I turned to look at Lewis, but he had broken out in a huge grin. "Joe Franklin! My God, but I once made a thousand bucks off of you." He walked to the man and shook his hand.

"You two know each other?" I asked.

"No," said Lewis. "Never met. But this is Joe Franklin from the New Orleans Saints. Center. Retired. Blew his knee out, home game against Tampa Bay Bucs."

"Nice to meet you," I said. I was completely confused, but then again, this was Lewis we were talking about. He invites confusion with the wily way he talks sometimes.

Joe Franklin smiled. He had the slightest of gaps between his two front teeth, which gleamed like a toothpaste-commercial smile. "We had a few losing seasons when I was with the Saints. You must have bet against the home team."

"Naw, not me. I bet the over-under. I would never bet against the Saints. And you were the greatest center in the NFL at the time."

"Thanks. Nice to be remembered. Well, listen, Mr. LeBarge—"

"Lewis."

"Well, Lewis…Ms. Quinn—"

"How do you know my name?" I asked suspiciously.

"I'm the founder, with my partner, C.C., of the Justice Foundation."

Now it all made sense to me. The Justice Foundation was a nonprofit group dedicated to freeing innocent prisoners through the use of DNA evidence.

"I'd like," he said, "to buy you both a drink and see if maybe you might see it in your hearts to help us."

I rolled my eyes. Where I come from, we know that if you're in prison, even if the charge is made-up, chances are you belong there anyway. The guy they originally thought killed my mother was freed when he came up with an alibi. But he was arrested not six months after his release for strangling his stepdaughter.

"I don't know." I hesitated.

"Well, I could always use a drink," Lewis said. "If you promise to regale me with the story of the time y'all beat the Bucs with that Hail Mary pass, I could at least listen to what you have to say."

"Deal," said Joe, flashing his megawatt smile. "Margaritas sound okay?"

Lewis nodded. "Man after my own heart. I like a nice tequila myself. Also like a smooth bourbon."

"He hasn't met a liquor he doesn't like," I muttered. Then I shrugged and sighed, but fell into step with Lewis and Joe. As we walked, I noticed that the massive man next to me was wearing loafers that had easily set him back a grand, and his pants had the crisp cut of an Italian designer. His leather jacket—which had to have been custom-made, given his ex-NFL build—looked butter soft.

"You went to law school after the NFL, right?" Lewis asked.

Joe nodded. "Blew my knee out, but they still had to honor the rest of my contract. I had invested wisely over the five years I played. Owned my place outright, owned my car. Didn't buy into the flash—except maybe for my clothes." He grinned, running his hands down the lapel of his jacket. "I drove a nice Mercedes sedan, not a souped-up sports car. I was set for life, as far as I was concerned. Invested in real estate, some solid stocks. My mama taught me very well. 'Don't be a flash in the pan, son,' she used to say. I was restless in retirement. She'd always instilled in me a love of reading and education so I decided to go to law school. After a couple of years with a blue-chip firm, I started my own private practice. I represent a lot of my old NFL buddies. Making almost as much as when I was with the league. But I started the Foundation because I felt that there were too many young African-American men in prison and that DNA might help get some of the innocent ones out. Since then, we've freed men of all colors and backgrounds."

I pulled my jacket tighter around me as a brisk wind whipped down between the tall apartment buildings. The sign for Coyote Canyon was lit in neon, with a giant green cactus sign jutting out over the door. The place used to be a hole-in-the-wall, before Hoboken became a trendy place to live back two decades or so ago. Yuppies started renting anything and everything they could find, hence Coyote Canyon became popular with the suit-and-tie crowd fresh off the commuter trains that hurtled beneath the river to Manhattan.

When we walked in, the hostess recognized Joe and pointed to a table where a woman sat waiting for us. We maneuvered around the women in Manhattan stylish clothes and the men with real Rolex watches on their wrists and sat down. Joe leaned over to give the woman a peck on the cheek first.

"Lewis LeBarge, Billie Quinn, this is Sister Catherine Christine. She goes by C.C."

The woman stood and smiled and shook each of our hands. She was stunning—and not dressed in a nun's habit. She wore a simple black turtleneck and black pants over black riding boots. She had a plain gold band on her left hand, and a simple gold cross around her neck with a diamond chip in the center of it. Her hair was long—and she had lots of it, in tight, strawberry-blond curls.

"Thank you so much for agreeing to meet with us," she said, smiling.

I looked over at Lewis, who was clearly captivated by her. He drawled, "May I ask how a nun and a football player ended up as partners?" He smiled as we sat down.

C.C. looked at Joe, who nodded.

"Well," she said in a soft, gentle voice. "I was in prison ministry…. I know it seems an odd choice, but I always felt like prisoners are the modern-day lepers. Forgotten, tossed away… And I met a young man by the name of Thomas Garson. He'd been railroaded into taking a plea bargain for murder two, but he was innocent."

"How did you know?" Lewis asked.

"Intuition. Prayer. Divine guidance. And I've been doing this long enough to smell the guilt on a man."

I tried to avoid laughing out loud. Lewis and I were creatures of science—and intuition and prayer weren't high on our agenda. Lewis was an atheist. I hadn't darkened a Catholic church in years. I understood what was under a microscope or in my test tube. I trusted traces of blood and sperm, or intricate patterns of crystallized drugs. Like most criminalists, I was a chemistry major in college, and I had my masters in molecular biology.

"Thomas was a fan of Joe's. His family had moved to New Jersey from Louisiana when he was a boy, but like a lot of people, he still rooted for that hometown team. Me? I could move to Alaska and still root for the Giants."

"A nun who follows football?" Lewis cocked an eyebrow.

She laughed and continued. "I promised to try to get him an autograph or a letter of encouragement. I'm sure Joe thought I was crazy, but I tracked him down. I hadn't realized he had gone into law. I told him about Thomas, and one thing led to another and Joe took his case pro bono and won an appeal. Thomas is now the file clerk for Joe's firm. Has a new baby daughter and a pretty young wife who's a paralegal."

"A happy ending," I said dryly.

C.C. nodded. "But for every happy ending, there's an innocent man languishing. More like ten innocent men. If they're of color or they're Hispanic or foreign-born, the number rises."

A waitress came over and Joe ordered a pitcher of margaritas and a basket of chips with salsa.

"No offense, Sister," I began. "But we just process the evidence. It's not for us to determine if some guy is guilty or innocent."

"Please call me C.C." she said. I wanted to

dislike her because she gave off an aura of such kindness my instinct was to think she was a fake, but I couldn't make myself. She just seemed that nice.

The waitress returned with a pitcher, four glasses and a basket filled with freshly warmed tortilla chips.

"Look," Joe said, leaning on the table with both elbows. "Walter Leighton used to advise us. But now that he's a super celebrity, he's forgotten us. We need you two to help us look at cases to see if there's even the possibility that new evidence might reverse a conviction or win a new trial."

"I always knew that Walter's swelled head would get the best of him," Lewis said.

Walter Leighton had written the forensic bible. When he consulted on a couple of really huge cases, his face time on *Court TV, Dateline, Primetime Live* and the *Today Show* increased until he was pretty much a household name and a celebrity. Then he had a ghostwriter pen two novels about a forensics investigative team and a police detective, sold about a million copies of each, and now he was famous and rich. Lewis hated the sight of Walter. I used to think it was professional jealousy. After I got to know Lewis better, I realized he saw the arrogance in Walter. It would be just like that guy to abandon the Justice Foundation. If Walter had walked away from C.C. and Joe, I knew just what Lewis was going to say before he even said it.

"We'll be happy to offer our professional opinions where we can," he said.

We. I'd gotten used to that, too. It was as if he thought of us as one person in that lab.

C.C. took out a folder from her briefcase. Her eyes were moist when she looked at us. "You have no idea how grateful we are." She absentmindedly patted Joe's forearm. "This work…it's our lives."

She slid the folder across the table.

Staring up at me from the mug shot was a man who made me blink slowly several times. He was beautiful. But beyond that, his eyes were soulful. Large and dark. He had a small scar on his left cheek, right near the corner of his eye, which brought my gaze to rest right at his pupils. His eyelashes were dark and made his eyes appear almost angelic. His hair was black and thick, with curl at the ends. He held up his processing number, and he looked stunned.

"What's pretty boy's story?" Lewis asked.

"David Falco is serving life for a rape-murder. The suicide king case," C.C. replied.

"I don't remember that one," I said.

"About ten years ago. A woman murdered in her apartment. She was an acquaintance of his. She was splayed out, and the suicide king from a deck of playing cards—you know, the one with the knife through the head—was left by her side. A knife had been plunged into her temple."

"Oh yeah." I nodded. "Now I remember." I had learned not to shudder anymore. Too many depraved cases.

"Evidence tying him to the murder?" I asked. For reasons I couldn't explain, I had a knot in my belly, as if I wanted to believe that the man whose face was so innocent-looking had to be, in fact, innocent.

"Not much. He admitted he had been in her apartment, so his fingerprints were there, but no fingerprint on the knife or the playing card. He was seen leaving her apartment in the window of time when she was likely murdered—but so was another man who was never found or questioned. David said the three of them had been hanging out together."

"So who was the other man?"

"He doesn't know. Said it was a friend of hers. But he never got the guy's name."

"Sounds fishy," Lewis said.

"I know," said C.C., "but there was possibly semen on her panties—panties lost by the police. The case was botched from the word *go*. And I don't know…he just doesn't give off a dangerous vibe."

"None of them do," Lewis said, pouring himself another margarita.

"That's not so. Even men who are innocent, after a time in prison, they start to smell of violence. They give off that feeling. But not him."

"So where do we come in?" I asked, still fascinated by the picture.

"Well, the panties surfaced after the trial in a paper bag in another evidence file. They were well preserved and I figure we have one shot at testing what may or may not be semen. I mean, we think it is. And we just need a break on this one."

I sipped my margarita and stared down at the picture. I wondered what the years in prison had done to that innocent-looking face.

Chapter 3

I drove a drunken Lewis home. He was a goner, and I don't mean just drunk—though he was that, too.

"Isn't she amazing?"

"Who?"

"Don't give me that—C.C." He pressed the electric button to move his seat way back in the car so he could stretch his legs.

I tried to avoid swerving off the road. "You can't be serious."

"What? You don't think she's beautiful?"

"Yes, I think she's stunning. She's also an N-U-N. Lewis...she's not available."

"I know." He smacked his forehead with his hand. "My luck I finally meet a woman besides you that I'm interested in and she's a nun. A beautiful nun, not one with a hairy mole on her chin."

"I'm not even going to ask why that would be your impression of nuns, because I'm sure there's some demented Lewis LeBarge story having to do with a decrepit old nun and I'm not in the mood."

"It's a good story."

"Save it," I snapped. "Lewis, be straight with me. Is the reason we're doing this consulting work revenge against Walter Leighton or is it because you've got a crush on a nun?"

"A combination."

"But it really has nothing to do with wanting to see justice served."

"Not really, no."

"You drive me nuts."

"I know. Listen, do you recall whether the lid was closed on Ripper's tank?"

About once a week, Lewis lost his tarantula.

"I think it was closed."

I eased my car into a space on the street.

"You want to crash here tonight?" Lewis asked, looking at me.

"As long as Ripper is in his tank, yeah."

We climbed out of the car and went into Lewis's house. I was tired, but I was still thinking about the whole crazy night. Lewis gave me a drunken hug, which for him also usually means planting a very loud kiss on my cheek—an exaggerated form of affection.

"There's pork rinds and Slim Jims if you're hungry, and your usual in the fridge."

"I'll pass on the snacks, but I think I'll have a Dr. Brown's."

I had long ago developed an addiction for Dr. Brown's Black Cherry soda—not always easy to find. The addiction was nurtured by my father, who used to take me and my brother to every diner between Rahway Correctional, where we visited my uncles, and home in Montclair, New Jersey, as well as every town we ever visited that had a diner, for that matter. Lewis always kept a supply of black cherry soda on hand, along with his sickening snack choices.

I heard Lewis climb up his stairs, and then I heard first one boot, then the other hit the floor as he pulled them off. I wandered into the kitchen and pulled a Dr. Brown's out of the refrigerator. I walked back into the living room. A soft chenille blanket was draped over the back of the very comfortable leather couch. I settled a pillow on the arm of the couch and took the remote and clicked on to Comedy Central. Part of me wanted to laugh. I popped the top on my soda and started drinking. It hit the spot, but then, like the soda often did, it made me start thinking about my father, my brother, my mother and me. It was entwined with my memories of childhood. And then, inevitably, I thought of the night she disappeared.

The lights of a cop cruiser reflected through the window and onto the walls of my bedroom. Red pulsated and filled my room. I rubbed my eyes and sat up as a police officer entered my room, the beam from his flashlight hitting my face. The cop lowered the flashlight immediately.

"Hey, sweetie," he soothed. "You okay?"

I nodded sleepily.

"Okay, then. You go back to sleep, honey."

"Is Mommy okay?"

"Why?"

"I heard them arguing."

"Who?"

I shrugged.

The cop came closer to me. "Think, honey. Can you remember what they said?"

I shook my head. "Where's Mikey?"

"Your brother?"

I nodded.

"He's downstairs with Officer Martin. You want to come down there?"

I nodded, and my teeth started chattering. Something was wrong, and I had no idea what. The cop came to my bed, and I saw the shadow of pity cross his face, a shadow I have learned to recognize many times since then. He scooped me into his arms and carried me down in my nightgown to the kitchen where my brother, Mikey, sat eating cookies with Officer Martin. They were dunking Keebler chocolate chip cookies into milk, and Mikey was talking a mile a minute.

I looked around the kitchen, teeth still chattering, and was handed a glass of Dr. Brown's Black Cherry soda in a highball glass with ice cubes. The officers asked me questions that I no longer remember. All I do remember is the look on my father's face when he got home that night.

She would never have left them alone, he screamed. He shouted what I already knew. In the instant I saw the red lights reflecting on my bedroom walls, in the moments of sipping Dr. Brown's, the bubbles tingling my nose, I knew. Whereas Mikey always had about him the belief that the world was a safe place, I knew differently.

Like Ripper on the prowl, even as a little kid
I knew that sometimes bad things escaped from
their hiding places.

Chapter 4

I spent that Monday at work testing a shipment of heroin to determine its purity level. Lewis called me into his office at around four.

"Here's the file on the suicide king case. We're supposed to look for something, anything, missed, in terms of DNA evidence."

"You looked at the file?"

He nodded.

"And?"

"And there was a tiny bit of what could be sperm on the panties. Too small to have been tested that many years ago."

"Anything else?"

"Well," he drawled. "I'm no lawyer."

I howled with laughter. Lewis's IQ hovered near 170, which I only found out one night over many shots of tequila and a poker game with my father, brother, uncle and Lewis. As I recall, I lost a bundle—and Lewis lost more. When Lewis lost even his watch that night, he bemoaned a man of his IQ being at the mercy of Lady Luck—and the Quinns. And he accidentally cited his IQ score. Like most geniuses, he could be prickly. And like most geniuses, he knew better than anyone else. And that included attorneys.

"And?"

"And the man had completely incompetent counsel, Billie. Guess who his court-appointed lawyer was?"

"Don't tell me…."

Lewis nodded. "Cop-a-plea."

Lewis and I may have been scientists residing in a world of DNA. However, we got to know the different cops and attorneys and prosecutors on the basis of their reputations. Cop-a-plea Fred? He had the worst rep of all. He had a serious comb-over, wore sweat-stained polyester suits, and bottles rattled around inside his briefcase.

"If Cop-a-plea was his court-appointed attorney, he didn't stand a chance in hell. Fred doesn't care about guilt or innocence, just avoiding actually showing up for a trial."

Lewis nodded. "This case is a textbook example of how to send an innocent man to prison for the rest of his life."

"So now what?"

"Now we test the tiniest of specks, evidence that was unable to be tested before. With the newer tests, I'm pretty sure if it's not too degraded, we can get results. Most of this guy's chances are pinned on that…we have to hope it's not so degraded as to be useless."

"Lewis?"

"Hmm?"

"You read the file, do you think he's innocent? Or are you still just doing this because you have a crush on the ultimate unattainable woman?"

Lewis didn't say anything for a minute. Then he swept a hand at his "wall art." His office also had crime-scene pictures, as well as some scientific prints of cells and blood under microscopes. "You know, it would be real easy, as a man of science, to remain forever detached from what it is we're actually doing. Over here—" his hand gestured to a crime scene with a body lying under a sheet "—we have the worst of what man can do. And over here—" he swept his hand to a cell photo that had been taken with an infrared camera "—we have cells, DNA and what they tell us. And never the twain shall meet. I mean, that's how it can be. We just remain in this world—the lab. We can be lab rats. But sometimes, maybe, we have to emerge and go into the other world….Yes, it's very possible he's innocent, Billie. And maybe it bothers me. And if I can do something about that, then I suppose I should."

"Dear God, does this mean you're getting a conscience?"

"Don't let it get out."

I knew, of course, that when the bayous of Louisiana released a floater who was once his childhood love he had had a determination to do right, using science. But I also knew he and I were both guilty of keeping our universe microscopic and not seeing the bigger picture. Maybe life was easier that way.

"Billie?"

"Yeah?"

"Do you think, if we do this, we'll be doing God's work?"

"I thought you didn't believe in God."

"I don't, but I thought…I don't know. Do *you* think we'd be doing God's work?"

"God and I are distant friends, Lewis. But yeah, maybe." I took the case file and turned to leave his office, and over my shoulder, I said, "She really got to you, didn't she?"

He didn't say anything, but Lewis LeBarge, the most rascally man I knew, definitely was doing some thinking.

My desk was piled three inches high with papers and files, and I sighed and looked at my watch. I'd be leaving after dark. The end of daylight saving time the previous weekend guaranteed that. I opened the Justice Foundation's case file and began poring over every detail. Police reports, evidence analysis, witness interviews. My heart raced a bit. I had to admit, like Lewis, that there was definitely something about piecing together a puzzle that was exciting.

Cammie Whitaker was the suicide king's victim—his only victim.

I took out a pad and pen and started writing questions as they came to me.

Why the suicide king playing card?
Suicide?
King = Power?

Cammie Whitaker was a beautiful redhead, a former college cheerleader for St. John's

with blue eyes and pale, freckled skin. In
her college yearbook photo there was an
aloofness, something unknowable to her
as she stared at the camera. In the crime-scene
photos, her blue eyes stared upward, and a
knife was plunged into her temple. Her body
was perfectly arranged, and there were thumb-
prints and finger marks in mottled red-purple
around her neck. She had been strangled, as
well. Everything else about her, though, was
serene. Her nightgown was beautifully splayed
out just so, as if, when the detectives walked
in, she had simply been sleeping.

Her apartment was in Ft. Lee, a town that
faced Manhattan and was an easy commute
from Jersey. Rents weren't cheap—and her
apartment reflected that. The place was stunning. The furniture was all French country,
tasteful. If they weren't actual antiques, they
looked like pretty good reproductions. She was
twenty-three. Pretty expensive stuff for someone that young.

Old money?

I looked through the file folder. Occupa-
tion...bartender. That place would need a hell
of a lot of tips, but then again, I tended bar at

Quinn's Pub every once in a while when they were short a bartender on a shift, or to cover for my cousins when they took vacation. I never ceased to be amazed at how much cash I took home.

I read interview after interview, some of them new ones done by Joe Franklin or C.C., about David Falco. Each one focused on how gentle he was, how he always took care of his neighbors—the kind of guy who, when it snowed, shoveled the walkways of the elderly woman next door as well as his own, throwing down rock salt and making sure there was no remaining ice that could cause her to fall. It was hard to reconcile that image with the one of Cammie, knife plunged in her head. Then again, my uncle Sean could regale a roomful of nieces and nephews with stories and amateur magic tricks, help us catch fireflies and give me a quarter for every A on my report card—and then go out and shoot a man in the head. I knew about men who could compartmentalize their family lives with their mob lives, keeping them separate.

I looked at photo after photo of David Falco, from his trial, his mug shot, family photos of him as a boy, as a teen. He was sent away when he was twenty-two. He had worked as a stonemason, and on the side he did restoration projects. He was apparently a very talented painter. Rough childhood, from the wrong side of the tracks, but he had made something of himself. Until he met Cammie Whitaker.

Lewis dropped by my desk. "Want to get a bite?"

"Nah," I said. "I want to go home and put on my pj's. I'm really beat. What time is it?"

"Seven-thirty."

"Ugh. Yet another twelve-hour day. How is it that you manage to work me like this?"

"You're in love with me." He winked at me.

"Uh-huh. Yeah, that's it…. Go on home, Lewis. I'll see you tomorrow."

"See you, Billie."

After Lewis left, I shoved the Falco file into my briefcase and grabbed the keys to my monstrosity of a souped-up Cadillac. I headed to the parking garage. My heels echoed on the cement. A few pipes overhead dripped dirty water.

My Cadillac was easy to spot. It even had a little orange pom-pom attached to the antenna that I kept forgetting to take off. I walked to it and inserted my key into the lock when I heard the unmistakable sound of a clip being inserted into a gun. I froze, my back to whoever had the gun.

"Turn around real slow, Billie Quinn."

Ordinarily, it *really* pisses me off when someone tells me what to do. However, a gun changes things in direct proportion to how likely it is I think the person might use it.

I turned around very slowly, my arms in the air. Whoever it was knew my name, so it wasn't a random mugging. When I finished turning around, I recognized the twin brother of Cammie Whitaker. I couldn't remember his first name. He had sat front and center at the trial and was in photo after photo. And he was the last person I wanted to see with a gun.

I nodded. "Hello," I said softly, cautiously.

His eyes were bloodshot, and I thought I smelled scotch. "You're a whore. You know that? You're a fucking whore."

I inhaled and tried to exude calm. "I'm sorry…" I struggled to recall his name. *Harry.* That was it. "I'm sorry, Harry."

"You're not." He started to cry, and the gun shook in his hand. "You're not sorry. You're working to free that freak from prison."

"How would you know that?"

"Those Justice Foundation people have been snooping around. I followed them. And now they've got you and that LeBarge guy on the case. Well, I'm telling you to drop it."

"Look, Harry... I can understand your pain—"

"You can't understand anything about that!" he snarled at me. He was a good-looking guy, but I could see the toll grief had taken on him. Whereas Cammie was forever twenty-three in death, Harry had grown older, and living without his murdered sister, coupled with, I guessed, alcohol, left wrinkles crisscrossing his face. His cheeks were mottled. His eyes empty.

"I can. My mother was murdered. And putting the wrong guy away for it isn't the way to peace, Harry."

"He's the right guy. The jury found him guilty in under three hours."

In my mind, I thought that was more a testament to his incompetent counsel than guilt or innocence, but I didn't say that to Harry.

"He may very well be the right guy—and science doesn't lie, Harry. People do. So if he's the right guy, the tests I run will tell us that."

Part of me understood Harry's reaction. Cammie's family, poor Harry here, had to live with the fact that if the cops had caught and maybe sent away the wrong man, then the real guy was out there—somewhere. If that proved true, who did they have to hate, to be angry with? If Falco was innocent, then they needed someone new to despise. That left the Justice Foundation. And now, thanks to Lewis's ego and his fascination with C.C., that left me.

"Harry...I don't know who did it. I just know that I want the truth."

"You see him?" His eyes were deranged. "You see him on TV? He never said anything. So quiet. Maybe a friend of his did it, and he stood around and watched. I get the feeling he'd like that."

Harry, his hair prematurely gray from the stress of his loss, his eyes sunken, started sobbing. I moved a step closer to him, and he cocked the gun and steadied it at me.

"No...no, you're a bitch. You don't care that my sister was murdered. That someone raped her. You don't give a shit about anything but proving your case. Being famous. You and those Justice Foundation friends of yours. You're all going to rot in hell."

"Look, Harry...put the gun down. You want to murder me? Will that bring back Cammie? Will imprisoning the wrong guy bring her back? Leaving him there won't bring you peace, Harry. It won't take away that gnawing panic inside."

"Bullshit."

"It's not bullshit, Harry. I know better than anyone that peace is elusive. And revenge isn't as sweet as people say it is."

Harry, his face ruddy from crying, rubbed at his nose. "Just leave the case alone."

Harry shook his head and then took his free hand—the one not holding the gun—and covered his eyes. And that's when I knew I had to move. I just didn't like the idea of my life being held in the balance by a man who was probably three sheets to the wind and grief stricken. So while Harry was distracted, I swiftly took my right hand and grabbed his, the one holding the gun. I took the palm of my other hand and smashed it against his neck, and then twisted his gun hand and forced him to drop the gun with a clatter to the cement floor of the garage.

Harry started to bend over to retrieve his weapon, and I kicked it under my car and then elbowed him with all my might in his ribs. My dad, when I became a teenager, insisted that I take a self-defense course. It was always there, unspoken between us, that what had happened to her could happen to me. I actually had a carry-and-conceal permit and could fire nearly as well as anyone I'd ever met at the firing range. The self-defense course, well…you can never replicate what happens when you really con-

front an assailant. But according to my instruct-
or, Mr. Ichita, my elbow-to-rib move could snap
a rib. Harry doubled over with a gasp. Perhaps
Mr. Ichita had been right. Harry was trying to
inhale, and I guessed the little popping sound
I'd heard was bone breaking. I brought my fist
down on top of his head and then backed up
three paces and took a running dive under my
car, retrieved the gun and commando-crawled
to the other side of the car, rolled out from under it and trained the gun on poor, bereaved—
and fucked-up—Harry.

"I'm going to pretend none of this ever happened, Harry."

He had thrown up on the cement of the garage floor, and slowly regained his breath. With
much grimacing he returned to standing position and looked me in the eye.

"Shoot me. Go ahead. Without Cammie,
none of it matters."

"Don't tempt me, Harry." The gun in my
hand was steady.

"You going to call the police?"

I shook my head.

"How come?" He looked shocked.

"Because, Harry…in the still of the night, I
know what it's like to wonder who murdered
someone I loved. My mother was murdered,

Harry. And her killer was never caught. So I get what you feel. I get that the last thought before you fall asleep, the first thought when you wake, is, 'What happened to Cammie?' To the point where you can't remember what she was like alive. She's a body in the morgue to you. She's someone screaming in the night for help. But I can tell you, Harry...putting away the wrong man isn't going to raise her from the dead. So your gun is staying here with me. Go get in your car. And if I ever see you around here again, I won't hesitate to kill you."

Harry's eyes widened.

"Do you know who Frank Quinn is?"

I waited while the name registered.

"The mob boss. Frank Quinn. He's my father. You ever hear of him?"

He nodded. In fact, very few people in New York and New Jersey *didn't* know who my father was. One of the last of the old-time mobsters.

"Yeah...Billie *Quinn*. That Quinn. Just means that me calling the cops over this incident would be the absolute least of your problems."

His bottom lip quivered, and he backed away. His eyes moved toward the gun, as if he wanted to take it back somehow.

"Leave it," I ordered. He nodded, then turned on his heel and ran, his footsteps echoing in the garage. It was dark out, the moon just a tiny sliver.

When he was out of sight, I opened my car finally, and slid into the front seat, the smooth dark velour soothing to my touch. It was only then, as I took the keys and started to put them in the ignition, that I began trembling. My teeth chattered, and my hands shook so badly I couldn't steady them enough to hold the keys. I leaned my head forward and felt tears drop from my face onto the steering wheel. What had Lewis gotten us into?

Chapter 5

"Collect call for Billie Quinn. To accept the charges, say yes at the tone," a mechanized female voice spoke. I waited for the tone and said yes.

"Hey, little sis."

"Hey, Michael. How's the inside treating you?"

"Two months and three days to go on my sentence. But who the fuck is counting, right?"

I laughed, hearing the cacophony of male voices in the background. "How's your roommate?"

"You always make it sound like I'm off at college…or camp. My *cell*-mate? He's got two years to go, but he's a mean gin rummy player. I'm into him for two cartons of cigarettes. But I'll earn it back."

"Even on the inside, you're always working the angle, Mikey."

"Always, baby. Always…God…" He paused. "It's good to hear your voice. How's Pop?"

"Daddy…you know, he's good. He's eating his way through the state of New Jersey—everything he missed while he was inside. Italian subs from Vito's, Aunt Helen's cheesecakes, the pub's burgers with fries and onion rings."

"You're making me hungry. I *think* we had Salisbury steak for dinner, but I can't be positive. The gravy had the consistency of Alpo."

My stomach churned at the thought.

"How was his homecoming party?"

"Awesome. Ended in a bar fight."

"As only the Quinns' parties can. That's the sign it was really good."

"It was the Murphy brothers."

"Shit." He sighed. "Poor Marybeth. Would you check on her for me?"

"Sure thing."

"You hear from Uncle Sean?"

"Yeah. I visited him a couple of weeks ago.

Brought him a picture of his Caddy. He misses the car more than me, I think."

"The fucking maroon land tank?"

"Yeah. He's okay. I promised him I'd drive up to visit him next month, too."

"Courtesy of the Quinn men, Billie, you've seen the inside of every prison from southern New Jersey to Dannemora."

"Dannemora is the worst. I feel like I'm going back to some medieval torture castle when I drive there." The Dannemora prison rose like a fortress in the mist in upstate New York.

"I'm sorry, Billie."

"For what, Mikey?"

"Everything. We should be protecting you, watching out for you. And we're all always on the inside, and you're alone. Spending your weekends driving to visiting hours and walking through metal detectors to make sure you ain't bringing us a file so we can escape."

"I'm a big girl. What else am I going to do with my weekends?"

"I have one word for you, Billie. A rather radical idea—it's called *dating*."

"Well, I am sort of seeing Jack again. Though he's pretty well sick of the fact that I spend my weekends visiting prisons, and I'm knee-deep in PCR tests and lab procedures.

Then again, he's a cop with a ton of baggage, so maybe we're a good match."

"You deserve a life, Billie. And this time, when I get out, I promise to keep my nose clean."

I looked at the picture on my coffee table of me, my long black hair pulled into a ponytail, wearing faded Levi's and a white T-shirt, no makeup, summer freckles on my suntanned face; Mikey, in jeans and a denim jacket, his black curly hair in need of a trim, his dimples cut deep into the hollows of his cheeks, his arm wrapped around my shoulder, head cocked to one side, lopsided grin as if he knew a funny story he was just dying to tell you; and Dad in his regulation orange prison jumpsuit, his hair cut prison short, graying at the temples, his face still unlined despite the life he lived.

"Mike," I sighed. "Don't make promises you can't keep."

He was silent. "You mad at me?"

"For what? Being who you are…? No, Mikey. I've never been mad at you for that. I'm not mad at Daddy. I'm not mad at Uncle Sean. I just worry. I don't want you to ever go back in, Mike. I miss you." I swallowed hard and wiped at a stray tear in the corner of my eye.

"Listen, the line for the phone is long. Let me go. Love ya."

"Love you, too," I said, then hung up. I looked around my apartment. A small one-bedroom, it boasted fourteen-foot ceilings with crown molding and wood floors. Were I a yuppie, I am sure the place would have looked fantastic with trendy furniture. Instead, it's an eclectic mix and match—homey and comfortable, but without any definitive style. My coffee table belonged to my uncle Mack—he's serving nine years in Sing Sing for racketeering. I had a really beautiful dining room table, too big for the space, which was where I ate and where I worked at night sometimes. Desk and table all in one. It was a beautiful cherrywood, from my cousin Joey, who had to leave town in a hurry. "I'll buy new when I come back," he'd said.

I had a nice television. I wasn't sure if it was bought legally or not. My dad gave it to me, and I've found it's much easier on my stress level to just not ask where his gifts come from. There's usually no taking them back—no receipts.

A few chewed cat toys were strewn on the Oriental rug that once belonged to Uncle Sean. My cat, a Siamese named Raphael, came over to me and slid against my leg, purring.

"Hey, baby," I whispered and bent down to

pick him up. I stood and walked over to the wall unit. It was cluttered with Quinn family memories. Every available spot of shelf space boasted a picture frame—photo after photo of my family—extended cousins and uncles included.

I went to one picture that was always front and center. My mother smiled out from the middle of the photo, Mikey on one side of her, me on the other. Her smile was openmouthed, as if my father, the photographer, had caught her midlaugh. She had on rose-colored lipstick, her hair long and framing her face. High cheekbones, blue eyes slightly upturned at the corners. My father never got over her death. I suppose none of us has.

My mother disappeared when I was nine. At first, the police wouldn't even investigate it because there was no proof she'd been abducted. They thought she had simply tired of being the wife of a mobster and had walked away. Eventually, they decided perhaps she had met with foul play, but by then the case was cold. And it wasn't until six months later that her body was found. A chain was around her body's neck— a neck that by that time was only bone. The case was never solved.

How would I feel, I wondered, if we found her killer after all these years, only to watch the sys-

tem release him? In that moment, I knew. Lewis
was my best friend, and I was all for freeing an
innocent man—if he was innocent. But I was going to have to meet David Falco myself. Face-to-
face. I was going to have to look him in the eye
before I stirred up the ghost of a murdered woman.

Chapter 6

I rolled over in bed and, sighing, stared at my digital clock. Midnight. I couldn't sleep.

Slipping out of bed, I pulled on my robe and padded into the dining area where I fired up my laptop at the table. I logged on to the Internet.

Out of the forty e-mails I'd gotten since the last time I'd checked, ten were spam. Fifteen were from my sometime boyfriend Jack; some were sexy messages telling me what he planned to do to me the next time we were together. One was from Mikey—he got to log on to e-mail every once in a while at prison. A couple were from Lewis. One was a ridiculous joke, solidifying my belief that he was several cornflakes short of a full bowl.

I clicked on my browser and plugged in "suicide king murder." Site after site showed up— crime Web sites. The Internet, I've discovered, besides being a playground for porn fans, is also filled with rabid fans of gore. The bloodier, the better.

I clicked on a picture of David Falco. He was wearing a prison jumpsuit in court. Lawyering 101 says have your defendant show up in a suit and tie. You can ask the judge if that's all right, and I'd never known a judge not to say a suit was allowed. Yet another example of his incompetent lawyer. I searched through the Internet for information on the case. The more I read, the more weary I got of the violence. I turned off the computer and opened my fridge. I poured myself a vodka on the rocks and drank it fast. I wanted to fall asleep. More than that, I didn't want to dream.

Because in my life, dreams usually lead to nightmares.

I don't know how C.C. does it every day. It's bad enough I visit prisons on the weekend. They remind me, most times, of the way I imagine insane asylums were two centuries ago. It isn't the drab walls and bars that bother me as much as the sounds of human misery.

When you walk into a prison, you hear the screams and yells of men in pain—either physically or mentally, or both. They scream because they don't want to be there, they moan and yell because they're crazy but aren't getting any psychiatric help, and they fill the air with filth—curses and expletives—because they torment each other with it. The entire experience is unnerving.

Three days later, after Harry's drop-by, I was ushered into a small conference room reserved for lawyers and clients. I waited a short time, and David Falco was shown into the room.

His pictures didn't show how tall he was—about six feet. He had the build of a quarterback, athletic but not hugely muscular. He averted his eyes as he slid into the chair opposite me. The guard left his handcuffs on and said, "I'll be in the hall."

"Hi, David." I smiled.

He nodded. His file told me he was thirty.

"I know C.C. told you we're taking on your case. Joe Franklin will be your new defense attorney. The wheels of justice grind slowly, so I can't say when you might expect results or even if we'll win. But you have my word we'll be relentless."

He was still physically beautiful. But his eyes had dark circles under them. I don't know how anyone sleeps in prison. You either learn to shut out the noise or you're perpetually sleep deprived. Or both.

"So what's your side of the story?"

He shrugged.

I knew that convicts closed themselves off. You had to do it to survive if you were a long-timer. The short-timers like my brother, my dad…they usually just got by with humor, making a few friends. But the long-timers were a different breed. I tried to imagine being in my twenties and drawing a life sentence—and being innocent. It would seem like a bad dream. A horror movie.

"Look…I know C.C. told you about me and Lewis. But I don't know if she told you who I am. Who I really am."

He looked down at the table. "I know who you are."

"Then you know about my mother. Look…I became a criminalist so that I could put the bad guys behind bars. I've never been involved in a case like yours. I never cared. I run a PCR test. I take a tiny little microscopic sample of human tissue, and I run tests. But I never put a face or a story to a sample before. And now…now Joe and C.C. came to Lewis and me. And they told us about you. But I have to see for myself, hear for myself, your story. Or I can't do this."

David Falco was quiet for a minute or two. Then he spoke slowly, carefully. "I told the story so many times, and it got me these." He held up shackled hands.

"But this time if you tell it," I whispered, "it might get you out of those."

His hands rested on the table, and I reached across and put my hand over the top of one of his. I gently squeezed and then withdrew. He clenched his jaw at my touch, and I just sat back and waited.

He stared down at the table, fixating on a spot. His eyes sort of glazed over, and he began to talk.

"I met this girl at a bar. I was working as a mason. A bricklayer. Followed in my grandfather's footsteps. He died after I came here. Anyway…saw her a time or two. She was… screwed up. Troubled. We never slept together. I…I was looking for a girlfriend, a relationship. Not a one-night stand. But I liked her, and I wanted to help her figure her life out."

I didn't take notes. I just listened. Jack, my sometime boyfriend the cop, said taking notes made people self-conscious. They froze up, and

I was certain if I took notes I wouldn't get the full story the same way I would if Falco was relaxed.

"Go on," I urged.

"Anyway, I'm hanging out at her house with her, after she got off work. This guy shows up. Never saw him before. Didn't give his name. I don't even have a good description. He was just average. Everything about him was average."

The way he said it, I knew that David Falco realized he was not average. He was very beautiful, and it had probably been a blessing and a curse his whole life. Outside, it had probably been a blessing. In here, a curse.

"Anyway," he said softly, "I just got this weird vibe. Like these two were into head games with each other, and I was just...being used by her. She kept calling him tough guy—not using a name. Mocking him. So I said I was tired and got up and left. I was there maybe five minutes with them. On the way out of her apartment, I passed a married couple coming home from a night out. They said hi. They id'd me the next day when her body was found."

"Can you articulate what was weird about them? About Cammie and this guy?"

"Articulate?"

"Explain."

"I know what it means. Just don't hear many big words in this place."

I smiled at him. "Sorry."

"It's okay. It's been a long time since I was treated like anything other than a dog in a cage…. I'm not sure what was so weird. I don't know. I mean…he stared at her like he hated her. And she was saying all this double-entendre stuff. Like implying he was inadequate in bed. I don't even remember. I was a little drunk, but I just felt like there was something going on there, and I didn't want to be around it. I wish now I'd never met her."

"Did you feel like…something sexual, like they wanted to involve you in something?"

He didn't speak for a minute or two, then he just gave me a single nod. "Maybe," he whispered.

"And you didn't want anything to do with that." I said it as a statement.

David Falco looked up at me. "No. In my whole life, I've been with three women. My high school girlfriend, a woman I met through my sister and a girlfriend who broke up with me maybe four months before the murder."

I found it hard to believe. My eyes probably expressed that.

"I swear to you. I was always a one-woman man. And I just didn't get into kinky shit." He smiled at me. "And to be honest, now it's been so long since I was with a woman, I can hardly remember." His smile was a little shy. And sad. "Anyway, this girl, Cammie, she had a dark side. Honest to God, I was trying to listen, to be a friend to her."

"Dark side, how?"

"I don't know. She was a bartender at this place I stopped in once in a while if I was working a job that way. We'd talk and later at night, when the place got quiet, she'd say things to me, like, 'You're so good, and I'm so fucked up.' But when I tried to tell her that she wasn't, that she could turn her life around, her eyes would well up, then she'd make a joke or something, or she'd go down to the other end of the bar."

"So why was she saying she was screwed up?"

"I never found out, but it always sounded big, like…something evil, or something really, really dark. I just felt kind of bad for her, this beautiful girl with some bad secret."

"Did any of this come out in the trial?"

He looked at me and shook his head. "My lawyer wasn't really interested in anything except maybe pleading me down to murder two."

"Can you think of any reason…any connection she might have had, to the suicide king playing card?"

"No. And trust me, I've had a long time to think about that. Nothing. I draw a blank every time."

"Did she use drugs that you know of?"

"No."

"Can you think of any reason why someone might try to frame you?"

"No. Look…before this, I was an ordinary guy. This has been like a nightmare I never wake up from. When I was first put in jail, I would have this split second every morning when I would think, for just this moment, that it had all been a dream. I'd be waking up with thoughts of taking the dog for a walk, and then I'd hear something, like some guy in the next cell, and I'd realize where I was. I wouldn't want to open my eyes."

I watched him as he spoke, his eyes radiating grief.

"I wanted to kill myself. I lost my will to live. I had a life, a job, parents who loved me, a grandfather who believed in me and taught me a skill. I had my painting, my dog."

"What kind of dog?" I asked, maybe for a minute looking to extend his memories and take him out of that prison.

"Oh." He grinned. "The biggest, sloppiest mastiff you ever saw. Name was Gunther."

"I have a cat. Siamese named Raphael. When I was a kid, my brother and I had a golden retriever named Honey." I didn't mention we got her after my mom died, to make us less afraid to go to sleep at night.

"After I got in here, my grandfather took care of my dog. 'Just till you come home,' he said. And then Gunther died. And then my grandfather died." He choked off a sob. "Do you believe I'm innocent?"

I nodded. I did. "C.C. is convinced of it. She says you've earned a college degree since you've been in here. Says she can tell you're, how'd she put it? Pure of soul. Says your writing is amazing. I'd like to read some of it sometime."

"After maybe a year, I went from suicidal to numb. And then I realized I'd have to find something to make me get out of that bunk every morning or I'd be living this horror show in excruciating detail until I finally died—alone. So I forced myself to take a correspondence course, to write letters to my parents. My dad's still alive. My mother got cancer three years ago and passed away. But my dad, he's the one who contacted C.C. and Joe. Anyway, it's not the exis-

tence I want, but it's better—that being a relative term in this place. I try to picture myself as
a monastic."

"A monk?"

"Yeah. I pray every morning. Buddhism. I
meditate. I let my meditation take me away
from here. But I just choose not to see a prison—to see a monastic life instead. I stay Zen.
But I'd still give anything to walk out of here."
His eyes were moist.

"I'll try."

I stood and called for the guard. David stood
and started to leave the room. In the doorway,
he turned and said, "Thank you." Then he left.
I gathered my briefcase and walked down the
corridor with a guard to the exit door, the bars
clanging open, then shut behind me.

I'd met men—friends of my father—who
had killed people and washed their hands and
gone out for supper. But C.C. was right. Whatever happened the night of the suicide king
murder, David Falco gave off the aura of a man
who wouldn't or couldn't harm another living
soul.

Chapter 7

On the way home, I pulled my Cadillac off the turnpike and meandered my way through New Jersey back roads toward Hoboken. I like back roads. I think better behind the wheel of a car.

I stopped at a Greek diner. My father's love of diners had rubbed off on me. Something about Greek diners, their menus as thick as novels with huge pages, and the ability to get pie or scrambled eggs at any hour of the day or night, made them seem magical to my little-girl eyes. Now I was all grown-up, and I still often stopped for a cup of coffee and pie or breakfast food late at night. I sat down in a booth in the back and ordered scrambled eggs and hash browns with a cup of coffee, even though it was long past dinner, without even looking at the menu. The waitress, all legs and frizzy blond hair, called back the order to the cook and brought me coffee. I stared into my mug, like an old-fashioned gypsy reading tea leaves.

Who was the mystery man in Cammie's apartment?

What was on her mind when she invited both men over at the same time?

What was the relevance of the suicide king?

What did a ritualistic murder imply about the relationship between Cammie and her killer?

What were her dark secrets that made her feel evil, compared to David Falco's innate goodness?

I ate my eggs, then I left and got into my car, driving down a narrow, two-lane country road. The sky was dark, and the road was unlit. I drove slowly, worried the light drizzle that had started would cause my car to skid on fallen leaves, as the trees were nearly bare.

The headlights of the car behind me were far off in the distance, and I wasn't paying attention. I was thinking. The next time I looked in my rearview mirror, the car was barreling up

and soon tailgating me. I picked up speed, and
the car picked up speed with me. It was a big
SUV, and I wondered if the driver was drunk or
in a hurry because of an emergency.

"Get off my ass," I muttered, feeling nervous. There was nowhere to turn off the road,
and I looked at my speedometer. I was pushing
sixty-five on a road that was slick. I should have
been driving thirty-five, tops.

I used my rearview mirror to check out my
road companions. The driver appeared to be a
man, but I couldn't be positive. I looked at my
speedometer again. Seventy. I had no idea what
Uncle Sean's Caddy could do, but even if it
could go 120 miles per hour—and it was a
smooth ride, I gave it that—it was still an un-
wieldy land tank.

The driver rode me still closer, knocking into my back rear bumper. My car started to fish-
tail. It then dawned on me the Caddy was a
"classic." No air bags. If this idiot forced me off
the road and I wrapped around a tree, I was likely to just end up good and dead. I wondered if
that was the plan. Had Harry followed me? I re-
gretted now not telling Lewis about the incident
in the parking garage, but I had assumed that
mention of my father would cause Harry to
think twice about messing with me. I couldn't

be sure it even was Harry. I felt at the end of our "conversation" that some of his rage had been spent. But who, then?

Ahead of me, I saw the lights of a convenience mart. I floored it. When I approached the store, I could see the parking lot was empty— who was out on a chilly rainy night but me? And the psycho in back of me. I cut my wheel sharply to the left and drove screeching into the parking lot, fishtailing nearly out of control. I slammed on my brakes and plowed out of the parking lot, up a curb and into a bush. I slammed against the steering wheel, and I thought I heard the blowout of a flat, but when the car stopped moving, I was still alive.

I opened the door and climbed out. The SUV was on the road, stopped, as if the driver wanted to see how I was. Maybe it was just a drunk driver, or a guy who got off on scaring women driving alone at night. That theory was blown to hell when the window rolled down and a bullet whizzed past me. I dived back into the car, and opened the glove box. I hadn't yet done anything with Harry's gun; it was still there.

Climbing back out into the parking lot, I held the gun, steadied it with two hands and fired off a shot. I hit the rear driver-side window and shattered it. The car sped off, the engine gun-ning as fast as it could. I hurried to the road and got the plates: JDV-611. New York plates.

A teenage boy in a polyester uniform poked his head out the door of the convenience mart.

"You okay, lady?"

I nodded.

"I'll call 911. I saw that guy fire at you."

"Do me a favor, kid, let me call a personal friend of mine. He's a cop. I'd rather he handle it, okay?"

The kid hesitated and then nodded and went into the store. I walked around the back of my car. I did have a flat. I took out my cell phone and called Detective Jack Flanagan.

An hour later, my Cadillac was being towed to a garage near my apartment, and Jack was yelling at me in the parking lot of the convenience store. I had woken him up—he told me he'd been dozing on his couch. By the look of his bloodshot eyes, I guessed that he might have had a stiff bourbon or two. He was wearing jeans and sneakers, and the most wrinkled flannel shirt I'd ever seen, with a denim jacket over it. His hair, dark brown with streaks of gray, was wet from the drizzle, and he hadn't shaved. He looked tired, and the crow's-feet around his eyes were accentuated.

"Let me get this straight. You didn't feel the need to fucking call me when this lunatic showed up in the parking garage with a gun."

"Correct, Detective Flanagan."

"Cut the Detective Flanagan crap."

"Look, Jack…he was drunk, he was upset…and I don't blame him."

"Give me a fucking break, Billie. Sure…I get it. He's upset that this guy may be walking, but you don't shoot the messenger, Billie. Killing you…what good would that have done?"

"Well, he didn't kill me."

"Only because you pulled all that karate crap on him—"

"Krav Maga."

"Speak English."

"I never took karate. I took Krav Maga."

"Fine. You pull your little Hong Kong Chop Suey on him—"

I shook my head. "Do you *try* to be this ignorant?"

"Anyway…you wrestle the gun away from him. Suppose you didn't?"

"But I did."

"Suppose you *didn't*."

"But I *did*."

He threw up his hands and turned his back to me, walked about ten paces away, and then came back. I'd learned this was a technique he had for calming down.

"Okay, Billie…so Harry ran away from the garage. You kept his gun. Today you head down to Rahway and visit the suicide king killer."

"No."

He sighed. "I'm trying here, Billie. You *just* told me, not ten minutes ago, that you went to see the suicide king killer."

"But he's not the killer. He's innocent."

"A jury of his peers found him guilty. Can we just *call* him the suicide king for a moment?"

I folded my arms across my chest. "Fine."

"And on the way back, when most *normal*— and I use that term loosely in any sentence associated with you—people would want to get home on a rainy night, you drive all over God's fucking creation in search of a Greek diner."

"Yes."

"Why? Craving a gyro or something?"

"No. They remind me of my father and brother."

"Okay, so moving along, you order eggs and coffee. You get back in your car. You drive all back roads. Someone comes and tailgates you. You assume it's a drunk. Until he forces you off the road and then fires a gun. You fire back, shattering the window, and get the plates. And now we need to pick up Harry, because it appears he still wants you dead."

"I don't think it was Harry."

"Well, we'll run the plates and see."

He stared at me. His eyes were a pale blue that, to me, looked perpetually sad. His only child, a little girl, had died of leukemia seven years ago—long before I met him. The strain broke up his marriage, and he took to drinking to get over it all. Add working murder after murder, and he was a cop on the edge. Part of me thought I even loved him, but he held on to his sadness, except for brief moments, and that sadness threatened to suffocate us both at times.

"Billie…I…listen, I can't have anything bad happen to you."

"Nothing will."

"You don't know that." He looked past me, out into the night. "Come stay at my place tonight."

"No. I have to feed my cat. Why don't you come stay the night with me?"

"Fine."

We walked to his car, a Chevy TrailBlazer with a hell of a lot of rust on it. We climbed in and drove in near silence to my place. We parked the car on the street maybe two blocks away and walked to my apartment. When we got there, Raphael meowed and came over to us. I reached down and scooped him up, giving him a kiss on the nose. Putting him down, I went to the kitchen and filled his bowls with food and water. I didn't offer Jack a beer.

"Make yourself at home," I called out.

I turned around, and he was right behind me. I jumped a bit. "You startled me, Jack. Why don't you sit on the couch?"

He didn't answer, but kissed me hard on the mouth, pulling me into him. His kisses are always hungry, the way a man who feels alone might kiss, as if he's somehow found an island to cling to.

My hands traveled up to his face. Next I wrapped my arms around his neck. Furiously, he unbuttoned my blouse, and I moved my hands down and undid his flannel shirt.

He cupped my breasts, still kissing me as if he truly *needed* me. We moved toward the bedroom. I unbuttoned his jeans, and we tumbled onto my bed. Wriggling out of my jeans, I was breathless. He climbed on top of me, his chest against me, and slid inside me. Finally, he stopped kissing me and moved his lips to my ear. "I would have died if anything had happened to you," he whispered, then moaned.

We made love, the fever building, until we

both came at once. He collapsed against me. That's how lovemaking always was with Jack. I rolled onto my side and allowed him to wrap his body around me. I felt a cold autumn breeze, and I noticed for the first time that my bedroom window was slightly open. I squinted in the reflected light from the streetlamps outside. Suddenly, I bolted upright in bed. "Oh, my God!"

"What?" Jack sat up, wrapping an arm around me.

"My laptop. It's gone."

Chapter 8

Joe Franklin and C.C. sat with Lewis and me in my living room over a good bottle of Australian pinot noir and a platter of cheese and crackers.

"Ever since I took on this suicide king case it's been trouble." I hadn't seen the point of filing a police report on my laptop—I knew the chances of finding the thief were slim to none. Jack had been both angry and concerned. I tried to tell him that it was no relation to the case, but we both knew that, at least on the surface, it appeared someone didn't want us digging around in the suicide king case. Dusting for finger-prints on the windowsill of my bedroom provided nothing useful—just masses of prints, mostly my own, since I used the window to combat the overactive radiator in my room.

"Nothing like this has ever happened before," C.C. assured me when she and Joe arrived the next night to discuss the incident.

"What was on your laptop?" Joe asked.

"Not much. I use it for e-mail and some Web surfing. I had recently done a search on Falco—but I didn't turn up anything anyone else doing a Google search couldn't come up with. Whoever took it doesn't know that. He may have assumed I kept a lot on it."

What I didn't say was I researched my mother's case constantly—all right, obsessively—but I always did a backup and stored a ZIP disc and CD-ROM copies of my work in a second location—namely a safe in Quinn's Pub.

"What did your detective friend turn up?" C.C. asked.

"Dead end. The plates, the car itself, appear to have been stolen."

"I'd say the real suicide king wants our boy to remain in prison," Lewis said.

"Either that or the brother is more nuts than I thought. I just didn't read him as anything more than a distraught relative who'd just discovered that there was a chance his sister's murderer might go free on a technicality."

"A technicality?" Joe said, a little irate.

"I don't mean it like that," I said calmly. "It's just that the average person has no idea of the accuracy of science. If people understood DNA evidence, then O.J. would be in prison instead of playing golf."

Joe Franklin shook his head. "Whether it's Harry or the real killer, it'd take a lot more than that to keep me from pursuing this—especially now."

"Well," Lewis drawled. "I'm rather fond of Billie, so much as I'd like to see your Mr. Falco released, I'd like to make sure we don't get Billie here killed in the process."

"Maybe we shouldn't have come to you. I never would have intentionally put anyone in danger," Joe said.

"The surest way to keep us *all* safe," I said, "is to process the DNA sample ASAP so the results are out there. The bottom line is once we have those results, whoever is looking to stop us will have to realize there's no putting the cat back into the bag. They could kill me or Lewis or you or C.C.—" I looked at Joe "—but it wouldn't change the results. Science always speaks for itself."

"Unless it's the O.J. trial," Lewis sniped, re-hashing another of his pet peeves. "Then some fancy-pants lawyer will find a way to twist the science into so much bullshit. Oh. Sorry about the lawyer thing, Joe. And pardon my language, Sister."

"Trust me, Lewis," C.C. replied. "You can't work a prison ministry if you have any sensibility at all about language. Besides—" she winked at him "—I think even Jesus Christ himself would agree there are some occasions and injustices when only a well-placed *f*-word will do."

Lewis laughed out loud. "A woman after my own heart."

I bet, I thought. I had never seen him so goofy over anyone.

"And I've heard every lawyer joke there is. But remember, I'm one of the few good ones. I'm quite concerned, though, because it seems like Billie's a target," Joe said, his rich baritone filled with worry.

"What about asking your father for a body-guard?" Lewis asked.

"No chance. I don't need some overgrown steroids-ridden leg-breaker babysitting me."

"Oh. Too late."

"What?"

"Too late. I already called your father and someone by the name of Tommy Salami is going to be minding you starting tomorrow."

"Lewis!" I snapped. "Give me a break. Not Tommy Salami."

"Sorry, Billie, dear. Your dad insisted, and I think it's a good idea. So we'll test the damn evidence and at least know where we stand. Until then, you get Tommy Salami."

I sighed.

Lewis gave me a dirty look. "I'm ignoring you, Wilhelmina, darling."

Joe howled. "Is that your real name?"

"No," I snapped. "It's Billie, for real—after my grandfather. But Lewis likes that little joke. Now half the lab thinks that's my real name.... Let me ask you, Joe, have you and C.C. ever taken on a case only to discover the man was still guilty as sin?"

C.C. nodded. "But only once. We get requests to look at cases every week—dozens of requests. From there we ask the person or his or her relatives or supporters to fill out an extensive form. I also meet people in the course of my ministry. Between the forms, phone interviews and my own contacts, we weed through and take a very limited number of cases, with the priority given to men on death row.

After a while, you do get intuitive about guilt or innocence. The guilty ones always have similar stories—it's never their fault, and by that I mean nothing is their fault. If they beat a woman but didn't murder her, according to them, even the beating was deserved—'But I didn't kill her.'"

"Charming," Lewis said sarcastically.

"Like I said, we've only been wrong once. And with David Falco, I'm not only one hundred percent sure. I'm one thousand percent sure."

"Well, DNA won't lie, so let's hope you're right,' Lewis said. "Let's hope this guy is worth all the trouble."

"I still marvel at the DNA aspect," Joe said.

"I admit that I still don't understand it completely," C.C. added. She picked up her wineglass and took a sip, her fingers delicate around the goblet. She looked as if she would be at home in a Botticelli painting, rather than a twenty-first-century murder case.

"Basically, C.C., DNA is like your own personal bar code." I used the metaphor I often utilized when I lectured at colleges on DNA technology. "Now, as humans, you and I and Joe and Lewis share certain DNA versus, say, a lion or a snail. We share our human DNA. But we have about three million base pairs of DNA that are unique to us—every person's is different except for identical twins. And so a person who leaves the tiniest of DNA fragments at a crime scene—under fingernails or a small swab of semen—leaves his or her genetic fingerprint. The problem—or actually, you could consider it a good thing if you feel paranoid about Big Brother—is that there's no massive database with everyone in the world in it. So there has to be a match with someone already in the system. If you don't enter the system and you fly under the radar, you won't necessarily get caught— unless you're a clear suspect."

"So why didn't they test this speck all those years ago?"

"Well, first it was lost. Then, it was too small. My guess is whoever raped Cammie wore a condom. This may have leaked when he took it off. Now we can use a technique called PCR— polymerase chain reaction."

"I don't follow," C.C. said.

"Years ago, we relied exclusively on RFLP, which required larger amounts of DNA, and pretty high-quality DNA at that," Lewis chimed in. "Now we can get by with a much smaller amount and duplicate it in the lab to arrive at our DNA fingerprint."

C.C. looked at Joe. "If the sample shows

he's not the man who left the sperm inside her, then what?"

"While they're testing the DNA, we'll be building on our interviews and trying to discredit testimony, along with the god-awful counsel he got. If the DNA fragment is enough to show he wasn't the rapist, coupled with the fact that he doesn't match the partial print on the knife—which the prosecution explained away as a latent print—it should be enough to overturn the conviction. He passed two lie detector tests, but the D.A. at the time was hell-bent on not having a serial killer case. He didn't want a panic in an election year. He wanted to close that case."

"Here's to DNA." I lifted my glass.

"Here's to Tommy Salami keeping you alive long enough to get it done, Billie Quinn," Lewis said as the four of us clinked wineglasses.

Tommy Salami was waiting for me the next day when I went out to my Cadillac.

"Hey, Tommy."

"Hi, Billie."

He looked about as wide as my car, and I could tell by looking at him that he was wearing a gun in a holster around his waist. His biceps, beneath a black leather jacket, were the size of my thighs. Tommy was an oversize pit bull who worked for my father, doing what I'm not sure and have no intention of asking.

"Do we really have to go through this exercise in stupidity?"

"Your father said I'm to stay on you like white on rice. Those were his exact words."

"Eloquent."

"Might as well agree, Billie. 'Cause you know I can't go back to your father and tell him I lost you again."

Tommy Salami—and Salami wasn't his real name, though I had no idea what was—had once been assigned to watch over me during an extended period of warfare with the Murphy brothers, in which it seemed they were smashing all Quinn cars with baseball bats and in general wreaking havoc in our lives. However, I was in no mood for any of it. So I gave Tommy Salami the slip—and my father was not amused.

"All right then, Tommy. Let's go." I opened up the Cadillac and climbed in. Tommy took the passenger seat.

"I'd rather drive."

"I'm sure you would, but it's my car and I'm driving."

"Mind if we stop for breakfast? McDonald's drive-through?"

"Nah. I don't mind."

I took Tommy through the McDonald's drive-through, where he ordered four Egg McMuffin sandwiches, eight hash browns, one large coffee and an orange juice. He munched away on breakfast while I drove to the lab.

When we got to the parking garage, Tommy made a move to get out of the car.

"Sorry, Tommy. Without one of these—" I pointed to my photo ID badge "—you can't come in. If you need the restroom, there's one in the gas station across the street. Good luck and I'll see you at six."

I wondered how long it would take for the coffee to run through him. It was also chilly out. I took pity on him and handed him my car keys.

"Here. You can run the heat if you need to."

"Thanks."

I climbed out and rolled my eyes as I walked away. I hoped the DNA replication would result in the evidence we needed. I wanted my old life back—and quickly.

Chapter 9

DNA kind of looks like a keypunch card once the X-ray film develops. In a sexual assault case, there's the victim's DNA, and then we also usually have DNA belonging to known people in the victim's life. For instance, if the victim is a married mother, her children's and husband's DNA would also be gathered so we would know whose DNA was also present at the same time versus the unknown assailant's.

David Falco had given DNA samples, and three days later, I looked at the way the tiny dots aligned after replicating the sample from the panties.

It wasn't a match.

I felt like screaming in the lab but contained myself. For verification, a second criminalist backed up my findings—Julio Chen. His mother was Mexican and his father was a Chinese dissident who'd defected when he was at MIT. Julio himself had gone on to study chemistry, and as soon as he finished his doctoral thesis, he'd have his Ph.D. in the same.

"Julio? You see what I see, right?"

He nodded. He had been following me every step of the way as I duplicated the DNA and ran my tests, watching me like a hawk.

"Not even close, Billie. This guy is not the rapist."

I held up my hand for a high five, rubber gloves and all.

"I've never seen you get involved like this."

"Well…this guy is special. At least the Justice Foundation thinks so, and I'm inclined to agree."

"You're lucky the sample wasn't too degraded."

I nodded. "That a little trace from years ago could come back and clear an innocent man is like out of sci-fi. I love what I do."

I stood up, satisfied.

David Falco had not raped Cammie Whitaker that night.

His prints weren't on the knife.

Nor were they on the playing card.

His attorney was an incompetent alcoholic who had since been reprimanded by the Bar four times.

Falco had passed two lie detector tests.

Every interviewee raved at what a great guy he was. That he was incapable of such violence.

I felt elated. In fact, though I had been a criminalist for years, I had never felt this surge of emotion as I processed a sample.

I went in to show Lewis the results. He acted underwhelmed.

"Come on, Lewis," I whined. "Be happy."

"I can't."

"Why not? I mean, C.C. will be thrilled," I teased him. "Isn't that at least a little reason to be glad about this?" I sat down in the chair opposite his desk.

Lewis stood and shut the door to his office. He turned around and looked at me. "Does the fact that you have to bring Tommy Salami to work with you three days running mean anything?"

I shrugged. I'd gotten over being annoyed.

"He's good company. And he's got nothing to do while I'm in here, so he details my car. Today he brought Turtle Wax."

Lewis shook his head and then went and sat down behind his desk, which was covered in file folders representing cases.

"If David Falco is innocent, as it appears he is, beyond a shadow of a doubt, then there is a suicide king killer out there. And he knows you. And C.C. And you're both pissing him off. Or else it's Cammie Whitaker's crazy brother. Either way, I don't feel too thrilled with this at all."

"You're just thinking of this now?" I asked. "What did you think would happen when we proved he was innocent?"

"I don't know. I've been a scientist for so long, I think I thought of this whole process in more abstract terms. Or more clinical terms. You know, on a microscopic level. Beyond that, before we started working with C.C. and Joe, we were faceless. Lab coats. We weren't targets. *You* weren't a target."

"We'll be fine, Lewis. We did something good. We did something that matters." I thought back to my organic chemistry classes and the endless science in college. I had done it because I liked science and I wanted to do something with it—law enforcement or forensics. But I didn't find myself necessarily excited by test tubes and Bunsen burners. This was different. It felt more meaningful. And if I was honest with myself, the thought of David Falco sitting across from me without handcuffs on was exciting.

"I cooked dinner for C.C. last night," Lewis said darkly.

"What? Lewis…she's a nun."

"It wasn't like that. She wanted a crash course in DNA, and I offered to teach her over a meal."

"Lewis," I sighed. I took a good look at him under the fluorescent lights of his office. He looked awful—dark circles, tired eyes, unshaven face. His trademark white oxford cloth shirt wasn't crisply dry-cleaned either.

"I can't help myself. We talk about God and chess—she plays—and childhoods spent in the country. She's from a small town. We talk about the bayous and about New Orleans drowning. And philosophy. Nietzsche and St. Augustine and St. Francis and Buddha…"

"Buddha?"

"She's got an amazing mind, Billie. We talk about everything and nothing. And…I'm being a good boy, of course. But it's killing me.

And even if I spend the rest of my life pining for her, just being her friend is good enough for me."

"How does she feel about Ripper?"

"She thought he was cuddly," he drawled.

"Lewis…you're going to make yourself crazy. I don't think this friendship is a good idea."

"Of course it's not," he snapped. "But neither is snooping around in old cases. I don't want the suicide king killer—if that's who's behind that attack on you—to harm her, or you."

"Why don't we have Tommy Salami watch over her? Would that make you feel better? My part is over, you know."

"I don't know if she would agree to having him follow her around. I mean, a nun and a… what do you call your father and his friends?"

"I call them Legally Challenged. It would just be temporary, Lewis. Come on, let's go out to the parking garage. We can at least talk to him about it before we mention it to C.C. and Joe. Come on." I was worried about ol' Lewis.

"Okay."

He stood, and the two of us left the lab. Going in and out we had to use a key card and a fingerprint match on a scanner by the door. The lab itself was as secure as Ft. Knox—or close to it. The last thing a prosecutor wanted was an

O.J. mess with accusations that the lab work was tainted or the specimen somehow contaminated. Lewis was known for running a very tight ship, with reason.

Lewis and I left the building and walked to the parking garage, which was owned by the city of Bloomsbury. Employees at the lab got a discount on the monthly fee.

We walked up the ramp, and I kept rubbing Lewis's arm. He may be the most annoying man on the face of the planet, but a depressed Lewis is even worse. When New Orleans flooded, he sank into a depression that lasted weeks.

When we got to the second floor, I made a left and then froze. "Oh, my God!"

"What?"

I pointed at my Cadillac.

The dome light was on, and there, in the front seat, was poor Tommy Salami.

Someone had shot him.

Chapter 10

Lewis grabbed me and pushed me to the ground. I landed on my elbow with a yelp. I pushed him away, rolled once and scrambled for my car. I knew Tommy was armed, and I wanted his gun. I also knew that except for the best SWAT team snipers, a moving target was pretty hard to hit.

"Billie, get down on the ground!" Lewis shouted at me.

My heartbeat raced as I dived for the cover of the car door. A bullet whizzed by my head, and I ducked inside. Then, gratefully, I saw Tommy was still breathing, albeit shallowly.

"Call 911," I screamed at Lewis. "He's still alive!"

I felt on Tommy's body for his holster and found his gun. I scanned the parking garage, looking for anyone running away, darting between cars—anything—but didn't see anyone. Then, behind a conversion van, someone ducked. I steadied the gun at the van. It was a hundred feet away and I had no idea what I hoped to accomplish, but I didn't want whoever it was to get away.

"Lewis," I called out, "there's someone over there. Come stay with Tommy."

Lewis dashed over and grabbed my shoulder. "Do you want to get killed? Stay here!" He had his cell phone out and was dialing 911.

I looked at poor Tommy, but I guess a combination of adrenaline and insanity took over because I shook off Lewis's grip and ran toward the van, ducking behind cars for cover. I began shouting at the top of my lungs, "Help! Help!" hoping that someone would come along to get his or her car and hear me.

A man wearing a dark blue hooded sweatshirt took off from behind the van. His back was to me, and I wasn't close enough to get a good look of any kind, especially with his hood pulled close around his face. He hopped into the passenger side of a four-door green Taurus at the end of the row, its engine running, and took off. I aimed my gun at the tires, but missed. At that point, some measure of caution caught up with me. I didn't want to risk a ricocheting bullet hitting an innocent bystander.

I tucked the gun in the waistband of my pants, and jogged back to Lewis, whose hand was pressed up against the bullet hole in Tommy's chest. I felt for Tommy's pulse. Still okay, if a bit thready.

"Come on, buddy, hang in there."

The bullet hole was about two inches above Tommy's nipple area, and it looked as though with every beat of his heart a little gush spurted between Lewis's fingers.

"Ambulance and cops are coming," Lewis said. I could hear the anxiety in his voice.

"He's bleeding bad," I replied, my own breath ragged with panic.

"Come on, ambulances," he said. "Maybe we should lay him down."

"I'm afraid to. What if the bullet is lodged in his spine or something?"

I heard the sound of sirens in the distance and let out a sigh of relief. Growing up with my questionable family, the sound of sirens usually made me feel a little nervous—all right, a lot nervous. But I was never so happy to hear them as at that moment.

An ambulance, a fire truck and three cop cars came barreling up the ramp in the garage in short order, tires squealing, sirens reverberating in the echoing parking garage, lights pulsating.

Two guys in blue uniforms hopped out of the ambulance and raced to us.

"What happened?"

"He was shot," I said.

"By who?"

"We don't know," Lewis said. "I'm Lewis LeBarge. I head the crime lab across the street. This is Billie Quinn, the assistant director."

"And this guy?"

I blurted out, "He's Tommy Salami. Um…I don't know his real last name. He's a friend of mine."

"Do you know his blood type? He's going to need a transfusion."

I shook my head.

"Do you know of any allergies to medications, any medical conditions?"

"No…oh, wait. I know he has high cholesterol and takes…crap, you know, one of those cholesterol-lowering drugs. We were talking about it the other day." I remembered mocking Tommy for eating his fourth Egg McMuffin before taking his medicine. He told me he had an aversion to fruits and vegetables.

"Okay, the police will talk to you. We'll take him from here." Lewis removed his hand and moved out of the way. The paramedics began working on Tommy, getting him on a stretcher and into the ambulance pronto, and taking off down the ramp, siren at full blast.

The police cordoned off the parking garage, and pulled Lewis and me to different areas to question us. I told them about the incident with Harry.

"How come you didn't report it?" a detective named John Fry asked me. He was young and good-looking—he looked as if he could have stepped right out from a cop show.

"I shrugged it off as a single act of grief. I wasn't hurt. I don't know...I just didn't think he'd really do anything."

"Well, looks like Harry Whitaker may have lost it big-time."

"I don't know. If he did, he had help." Someone else had driven that car.

In the midst of all the chaos, I managed to call Jack. He arrived with his new partner about a half hour later and started buddying up to the various police on the scene, smoothing things. Next thing I knew, I was "free to go."

Jack pulled me to the side. "You done with this?"

"Now I am. We got the results today. He's innocent."

"I mean these Justice Foundation people. Maybe the next time you clear some guy for murder you won't be so lucky."

"Look, I still have to call my father, and then there's Lewis over there. And I'm sure it's just a matter of time before my brother calls me *collect* to nag me. Not you, too, Jack."

He shook his head. "We'll discuss this later. Vic and I have to wrap some things up on a case. I'll call you tonight."

"Can hardly wait," I said sarcastically. Then I stopped. "I'm sorry. Thanks for all your help, Jack. I mean it."

Jack took off with his new partner. His old one had had a heart attack about six months before and ended up taking early retirement.

After the police finished questioning me, I called my father so he could notify Tommy's family that he'd been shot. I was standing in the lab parking lot with Lewis, whose shirt was covered in blood. My car had been impounded as evidence by the police. I was shivering in the cold—and from nerves.

"Billie," Dad said. "Jesus Christ…is Tommy going to be okay?"

"I don't know, Dad."

"It could have been you."

"I know."

He was quiet for a moment or two. "I almost didn't survive losing your mother, Billie. Be careful. Have Lewis take you home."

I closed my cell phone. "Well, Lewis, I don't know about you, but I'm ready to take a hot shower and go to bed."

"Is that a come-on?"

"Shut up."

The two of us walked to his car, a much-driven and much-loved classic Thunderbird in sky blue that Lewis had owned since college and restored and kept up himself. We both climbed in and I leaned my head back against the seat.

"Can we not talk about this, Lewis?" I begged, heading him off.

He sighed. "Sure thing."

"I can't believe you're not arguing with me."

"I felt a man's life pulsing through my fingers tonight. I may have left academia for the lab, but…this was heavy. I need a stiff bourbon."

"Me, too. Come on, drive me home and we'll have one together."

We drove to my place, and while I got out

two glasses and ice, and bourbon from my cabinet, he borrowed one of my brother's sweat-shirts that I'd somehow kept over the years, and took a shower and changed. I poured us both a glass, and set them down on my coffee table. He sank into my couch and turned on the television.

"Think your father can get me a deal on a flat screen like yours?"

"As long as you don't mind the no-receipt thing, Lewis."

"I'm getting used to such concepts." Lewis's father was a retired judge in New Orleans, his mother a lifelong homemaker and member of the Junior League.

"I'm going to go shower."

In my small bathroom, I turned on the hot water in the shower and climbed in, letting the steam rise and the hot spray hit my back where the knots of tension were. I stayed in there until the water ran lukewarm, then started to get chilly.

I climbed out, toweled off, combed out my hair and pulled it into a ponytail. I pulled on a pair of sweatpants and a rugby shirt, which had also been my brother's. Then I went out to the couch. Lewis was watching Nickelodeon.

"Can I ask why we're watching *Sponge-*

Bob?" Lewis was a major newshound, and it was usually the History Channel, CNN, MSNBC…or something on PBS.

"I tried the news. We're on it."

"Ugh."

"Precisely. So we're watching *SpongeBob*."

"Here's to the pineapple under the sea." I took my bourbon and clinked glasses with him. "We should call Joe and C.C. They'll be worried."

He nodded.

"Lewis?"

"Yeah?"

"Do you really think the true killer is after us, or do you think this is Harry Whitaker?"

"I don't know. I just regret bringing you into this, Billie."

"Lewis…when have you ever known me to listen to anyone anyway? If I didn't want to be involved, I wouldn't be."

I reached for my portable phone and dialed Joe.

"I've been sitting here waiting for one of you to call," he said. "You all right?"

"Yeah. We're both okay. A little rattled, but okay."

"And the DNA?"

"Not a match."

I heard Joe let out a whoop on the other end of the phone and relay the message to C.C.

"I can't wait to tell David."

I smiled. "Let me sign off. Lewis and I are wiped out."

"Okay. Take care. Stay safe."

"Thanks."

I hung up and looked over at Lewis. He was sound asleep. "Poor baby," I whispered. I went and pulled the comforter off my bed and wrapped it around him.

"Good night, Lewis." I turned and went to bed and tried to fall asleep. But my mind was cluttered with thoughts of the suicide king killer. I was happy that David Falco was cleared, but now I wondered who really had murdered poor Cammie.

Chapter 11

Tommy Salami should be grateful he's a steroidhead. Layers of muscle trapped the bullet before it hit his heart. He was hurt—badly—and he lost a lot of blood, but the doctors said he would be okay.

The next morning, Lewis went home, and I made a pot of coffee, called the hospital to check on Tommy and made scrambled eggs on toast.

My phone rang halfway through breakfast and I picked up.

"Collect call for Billie Quinn from David

Falco. To accept the charges say yes at the tone."

After a moment of shock, I said yes. I wondered, not for the first time, what the phone company thought seeing all those collect calls I received from different prisons.

"Hello?"

"Billie?"

"Yeah. Hi, David. I guess you heard the good news—not a match."

"I know. I'm still sort of numb. I'm sorry for calling collect. I got your number from C.C. I begged her for it. I just wanted to thank you. You could have refused to work on my case. You could have decided you didn't care. I know you took this and made some sacrifices. I heard about your friend."

"He's going to be okay, thank God. Officially, at least for right now, because he, in police parlance, 'consorts with known felons,' they've tied it to his own background and not your case, which is good for you. I think it's best if the pure science and DNA clear you rather than muddying up this case with a lot of things we can't prove. Better to go with what we can prove— which is that your DNA wasn't on the victim."

"I'm glad your friend will be okay." He hesitated. "Is he your boyfriend?"

"Um, no. He does some work for my father occasionally. I think Lewis, my boss, was worried after my apartment was broken into. So my dad sent Tommy Salami over to watch me for a few days. I don't know…maybe it's all coincidence."

"I hope so. I promise when I get out of here and get a job that I'll buy you a new laptop to replace the one that got stolen—Joe told me."

"Don't worry about it. You just get the hell out of there. I have a desktop computer. I'm okay. I'm still getting e-mail."

"You are? Can I write you?"

"Write me?"

"An e-mail. When you came here, you said you wanted to read some of my writing. I thought maybe I could send you something."

"I'd still like that. My e-mail address is bquinn5559@hotmail.com."

"I want you all to know how much I appreciate what you've done for me. I can never repay you."

"Honestly, I can't tell you how it felt to look at that film and see that it wasn't a match."

"I told you I was innocent. To prove it now… I'm afraid to believe, but there's this tiny little bit of me that thinks this nightmare might be over."

"C.C. was the one who really started this. She never stopped believing."

"Billie…my grandfather never stopped believing in me. My parents. But when C.C. and Joe and you believed in me, it meant even if I died in prison, in some ways I wasn't alone. Thank you." His voice cracked.

"It's okay, David. When you get out, we'll have a big party."

"Big parties aren't my style. I'd be happy with a quiet dinner where I could get to know you—and C.C. and Joe. And Lewis. I hear he's a character."

"Yeah, that's a pretty good description of Lewis."

"Well, I better get going. I've got ten guys here waiting for the phone. Thanks again. I mean it."

"You're welcome."

After I hung up the phone, I went over to my briefcase and took out the Falco file. I laid out a couple of pictures of him on my dining room table and looked down at his photos. I wasn't sure what it was about him that was so intriguing. Maybe it was the way he carried himself. He had been locked up for years, falsely imprisoned, and yet he hadn't let it destroy him. That was a rare form of courage. And he was, unmistakably, interested in me.

* * *

Dear Billie,

I used to hate going to sleep. I used to have this recurring nightmare. I was being strapped to a gurney, ready for my execution, and they were approaching me with the needle. In the gallery, I could see my father—and my mother and grandmother and grandfather. All the people I have ever loved, who ever cared about me. They could hear me if I said something to them, but I couldn't hear them. I was lying there, seeing my mother gripping her chest in pain, sobbing, soundless, wordless, and I was powerless to stop her pain. That hurt more than being in this place. I dreaded sleep.

I wasn't given the death penalty in reality, but prison is its own death penalty if you are innocent, sucking the life from you slowly, bit by bit, day by day. Then there were nights, I told you, when I would dream I was free. The crushing pain when I woke up would be physical. Like a cinder block on my chest.

Now, I have this tiny little glimmer of hope. It's like that first breath when you dive deep into a lake and come up to the surface. You gasp for that first bit of air, so sweet and cool on your face. So now, when I go to sleep, I shut my eyes, and I meditate like always. I take myself out of these prison walls, but now I picture myself standing on a mountain as fresh snow falls. It's all quiet and hushed, the snow muffling all sound. And then I see you making snow angels. I go and I lie down next to you and we look up at the sky. The sky is different in my dream. You know that you take freedom for granted. I did. In here, in the yard, even if it snows, I look up and always see the same patch of sky, the same view. In my dream, I can stand on the mountaintop and spin in a circle and see new sky, a horizon, as far as my eyes will take me. The air is free air.

I hope I don't make you uncomfortable—that's never my intent. I don't have any expectations of what this friendship will mean once I'm released—if I'm released. But I wanted you to know that for all those years in here I was afraid to dream, and now I'm not. And for that reason, you'll always be a part of me, however our paths diverge from here.

Thanks, Billie. And thanks for your letters and the books. I look forward to hearing from you. I like the stories you write me about Lewis and the lab—and your family. It takes me out of here for a little while and puts me back into a world I hope to one day rejoin.

    Fondly,
    David

Joe Franklin worked fast. From his own pocket, he hired a full-time paralegal devoted solely to the Falco case. Joe filed immediate emergency briefs, and he and Lewis went on talk shows to eloquently present the evidence over the next few weeks. Lewis was becoming as famous as his nemesis, Walter. And with each day he was growing closer to C.C.

Harry Whitaker had an airtight alibi for the shooting in the garage, and so the case stayed unsolved—but since no other incidents occurred, we all relaxed and assumed it had nothing to do with the Falco case.

David continued to write to me from prison, long, beautifully eloquent e-mails that spoke of the inner journey he had taken. Beneath the surface of a prisoner in an orange jumpsuit was a man with a deep spiritual and intellectual capacity. I sent him books he requested on Gandhi and Nelson Mandela. On men who had risen like phoenixes from the ashes of difficult circumstances.

And on Christmas Eve, with press cameras flashing, David Falco walked out of prison a free man into the embrace of his father, who had never stopped believing. Joe had two limousines waiting. One for David and his father—with champagne chilling—so they could enjoy the freedom ride together, and one for the Justice Foundation team—Lewis and me, C.C., Joe and the paralegal, Alex Lopez, a tough kid from the Bronx, whom Joe had taken under his wing and helped to turn his life around.

In our limo there were also a couple of bottles of Cristal. Joe, I had discovered as our friendship grew, was a hardworking attorney, but when it came to entertaining, a bit of his old NFL flash came out.

We lifted our flutes of champagne in a toast as the driver started on the Garden State Parkway back toward northern New Jersey.

"To David Falco," C.C. said.

"To the Justice Foundation," Alex chimed in.

"To friendship," Lewis said. "And to the New Orleans Saints."

I sipped my champagne and then said quietly, "What do you think his adjustment is going to be like? I can't imagine emerging from prison after ten years. Think back ten years. All those experiences, all that time I threw away and never appreciated. Every day I woke up free was a gift. Think of who you were ten years ago. Think of the way the world has changed."

C.C. nodded. "The Foundation will do its best to help him, but it's always tough for these guys. There's the honeymoon period. Eating all the foods they love and missed. Drinking a cold beer. Sleeping in a bed with crisp, clean sheets and no cellmate snoring in the bunk above them. But then, they have to go through a grieving period, and in some ways that's more brutal than the time spent in false imprisonment."

Joe said, "We see it with each guy. They go and look up old friends, they see their brothers and sisters. And what has happened in ten or fifteen years? Well, the world has gone on. Their friends have married, their brothers and sisters have children. They have houses and jobs—all the things that the prisoner never had and may never have. The waste of those years is a huge psychological toll. One guy—you may have heard of him…Rick Sparkhill, the guy who was cleared of that rape-murder in Seaside Heights at that motel—he attempted suicide."

"So David has a tough road ahead of him," I said.

"Yes, but he has a few things going for him." C.C. tucked a stray curl behind her ear. "First of all, he didn't waste his years in prison. He got a degree, he started and wrote for the prison newspaper, he read, he fostered friendships. He embraced Eastern philosophy. He didn't stop growing as an individual, even as this horrible miscarriage of justice left him somewhere he never should have been in the first place. Our research indicates men who do what David has done fare better upon release. Also, because the case seemed to highlight the worst of the justice system—an incompetent public defender and all that—he has some notoriety. A good kind. People believe he is innocent. A couple of messages have come to the Foundation, offering him jobs. With other guys, sometimes ignorant people just don't believe the science."

We rode on, arriving around six at Joe's magnificent mansion in Alpine, New Jersey. It had a long, sweeping driveway, and the path to the ten-foot-tall double wooden doors, carved with a dragon on the front, was illuminated with small Japanese-style lanterns.

We got out of the limos and walked into the house. Joe had hired two waiters, a bartender and a chef for the evening. Glasses of champagne were handed to us, along with hot hors d'oeuvres.

We toasted David's freedom again, and ate puff pastries and mushrooms stuffed with crab-meat. At one point, David came to me and we walked together into the study.

"I'm numb," he said. "Numb and overload-ed with food and alcohol at the same time. I haven't eaten like this in ten years. Pinch me. Tell me I'm not dreaming. That I won't wake up back in my cell."

I thought he was kidding, but his eyes were earnest, desperate almost.

Playfully, I pinched his bicep. "You're not dreaming."

He grabbed my hand and squeezed it. "Thanks." I felt a surge at his touch, but we just turned and went back to the party.

Beneath the tall, full Christmas evergreen in Joe's living room sat a few presents from us to David—clothes, books, a warm sweater and a new pair of shoes.

He opened two from me, a first edition copy of Albert Camus's *The Prisoner*, and a book by Thich Nhat Hanh, a Buddist monk David ad-mired.

"Thank you," he said, swallowing hard. He looked at me intently, but then C.C. thrust another package at him, then another.

He smiled bashfully and opened them all, shaking his head from time to time. "You guys are unreal. My freedom was present enough."

Joe's chef put out a spread of Kobe beef, sushi, baked brie and cold smoked salmon with capers and onions. It was an incredible buffet. We drank bottle after bottle of champagne.

Around midnight, my cell phone rang. I saw from caller ID that it was Jack. I excused myself and stepped into Joe's study to take the call.

"Still with the suicide king?"

"Jack...stop that."

"You should be home with me for Christmas Eve."

He slurred the *s*'s in Christmas.

"Jack...are you drunk?"

"What do you care if I am?"

"I care because you've been blowing off your A.A. meetings again."

"Fuck off. I read his letters. He's in love with you."

"My letters? Where are you?"

"Your apartment."

"You read my letters? I thought you were spending Christmas Eve with your partner."

"We did. Now I'm here. Waiting up for you."

"Snooping is more like it. You're a son of a bitch, Jack." When he drank, he could be nasty. And now, I guessed, devious. I had printed out David's letters and saved them in a box, in the file cabinet where my mother's case clippings and files were.

"Trust me, Billie, like all ex-cons, even if he didn't kill that girl, he's trouble. I give it a couple of months before he's arrested for something else. And maybe your intentions toward him were all good. Clear an innocent man, help mankind—whatever, Billie. But I read his letters. He's playing you."

"He's never said he loves me in those letters, Jack. He's simply reaching out to a friend."

"Friend, my ass."

"I'm not going to listen to this, Jack."

"No job, no home, no money. He was probably released with about a hundred bucks from what he made at a prison job making license plates. He needs a place, clothes, a good lay. Money. He's playing you for all of that and you're too blind to see it."

"I see one thing. That the only time I've been a poor judge of character was in getting involved with you. Merry Christmas. Hope you enjoy spending it alone."

I pressed End and folded my cell phone. That was it. Jack and I were over—and part of me was relieved. I'd have to change the locks on my place. Tonight I'd go home with Lewis rather than risk running into Jack. I felt sick to my stomach and tried to shake it off.

I rejoined the party. David was, at that moment, talking to Lewis and laughing. Everyone was in the soft glow of Christmas lights. A fire was in the fireplace. Christmas music was playing on the stereo. I felt peaceful.

We had really done it. The Justice Foundation had freed an innocent man.

But then I wondered if the ghost of Cammie Whitaker would let us rest without finishing the job. Without finding the real killer.

Chapter 12

My father and Lewis changed the locks on my apartment, and two weeks later, we were having yet another Quinn homecoming party, this one for my brother, Mikey. I hoped we could manage the evening without a bar fight.

I invited Joe, C.C., Lewis and David to the party at Quinn's Pub. My uncle was a little shorthanded, so I was actually working the bar when the four of them came in together.

In the short time since his release, David had moved in with his father until he got on his feet. He had bought a new wardrobe, cut his hair and spent long days hiking in the woods. His father's homecoming gift to him was a puppy. It seemed such a little boy thing, but I know it was the best medicine—not a replacement for the dog that died while he was in prison, but a new start. He named the dog Bo, and took him out in the snow. Took him nearly everywhere.

All that fresh air meant David had lost his prison pallor and looked healthy. He was also entertaining a book offer. We were encouraging him to take it—not only would the money help him start a new life, but we also felt it would bring valuable attention to the plight of the wrongfully convicted. Contrary to my father's wishes, I decided to continue my association with the Justice Foundation. So did Lewis— though *his* reasons were hopelessly transparent.

"Hey, guys!" I waved as the four of them walked into the bar.

Joe grinned. "Billie Quinn tending bar. This I gotta see."

Lewis said, "Don't let that lab geek act fool you. She's awfully comfortable back there. She'll pour you a beer with the perfect foamy head on it, mix you a margarita, or make the driest and most devilish martini. Name your poison."

"Scotch on the rocks for me," Joe said. "Single malt."

I grinned. By now I had gotten used to Joe's refined tastes.

C.C. wanted a glass of chardonnay, and Lewis had a bourbon on the rocks.

"I'll take a bourbon, too," David said.

As I put the last of their drink orders on the bar, I said, "They're playing pool in the back. And in the party room there's a game of high stakes poker."

Joe raised an eyebrow. "I could be persuaded to play."

"Which?" asked Lewis.

"Either."

"You any good at pool?"

"I was the best pool player on the Saints in my time."

Lewis wrapped an arm around Joe's wide shoulders—which, despite Lewis's height, required stretching a little. "Can I persuade you to be my partner and shoot a game of pool against Frank Quinn? Billie's father has been a thorn in my side for long enough. I could use a little help."

"Sure thing."

"Be careful, Joe," I warned him. "My father's a hustler at the table."

"I think I can handle it."

"All right. Don't say I didn't warn you."

"Smell the air," Lewis commanded. "What do you smell?"

"Beer?" C.C. guessed.

"No. I smell victory. Come on, Joe. To the tables."

C.C. shook her head but followed the two of them to their certain doom at the felt billiards table. That left David sitting at the bar across from me.

"You look great, David. Well rested."

"Thanks." He grinned and patted his stomach. "Have to say that freedom agrees with me. My father and my aunt and uncle have been cooking for me, breakfast, lunch and dinner. I've packed on ten pounds."

"It agrees with you."

"You look beautiful, Billie."

"I look sweaty and I smell like beer, but if that's your kind of gal…"

"You're my kind of girl."

I blushed and moved down to another reveler—one of my brother's pals. It was shaping up to be another Quinn family classic. The place was packed, and we were going through beer as if it were water, and cases of Jameson whiskey. But every couple of minutes, I'd glance down at David. He had told C.C. and me that he was still learning to accept his freedom. He was often in a state of hyperalertness, getting used to not having to watch his back and fear prison violence. Getting used to the noises on the outside. Better yet, getting used to being alone. He no longer needed to travel inward to find solitude; he could take long, contemplative walks.

About forty-five minutes later, the regular bartender, Shelley, came in. She was a third cousin of mine. She took over, and I joined David on the other side of the bar. We sat next to each other on stools and ate peanuts and drank bourbon. At some point, he took his index finger and stroked the top of my hand. I felt my breath catch, then he took my hand and clasped it, resting both our hands on his thigh.

"Want to go watch Joe and Lewis lose?" I asked.

"Wouldn't miss it," he replied.

We went, hand in hand, back into the poolroom, and sure enough, ten minutes later, my dad and brother won, and Lewis and Joe each handed over twenty bucks.

"Man," Joe said, opening his wallet. "I'm going to practice and come back and kick some ass."

"That's how they rope you in, sucker." I laughed.

Marybeth Murphy sneaked behind my brother and squeezed his waist. He whirled around and kissed her. He had loved Marybeth since high school, and one of these days, I expected them to make it legal. Which, given my brother's long rap sheet, would likely be about the only thing legal in his world.

The night wore on with more laughter and a lot of gambling, drinking and old-fashioned Quinn fun. A craps game started in the back. I blew on the dice for my brother, and he ended up winning a few hundred dollars. We closed the place around three—with no surprise visit from the Murphy brothers. All in all, a good night.

My dad came over to me and kissed me goodbye. He was very busy with football season—a bookie's busiest time of the year. Lewis, Joe, C.C., David and I helped put up the tables, stacking chairs on top of tables so that in the morning the cleaning crew could come and mop. My uncle was counting up the night's receipts in the office. My guess is he'd report a very small fraction of the business we did.

The television was on and my brother shouted at Shelley to change to CNN so he could see the hockey scores.

Suddenly, C.C. screamed and literally grabbed on to a table to steady herself.

I looked up at the television to catch the anchor's report.

"And in a shocking twist to the release of inmate David Falco, a woman was murdered tonight in Atlantic City, New Jersey. Anonymous sources tell CNN that the crime included a playing card left at the scene, leaving sources to speculate on a copycat killing. This is a developing story and we'll bring you more as soon as we have information."

My breath left me, and my legs trembled. The suicide king had struck again.

Chapter 13

Joe called a friend of his in the police department—a cop who moonlighted for him doing security from time to time. The guy was helpful. The murder had taken place, according to the M.E.'s preliminary, that evening. David had an alibi. He couldn't have murdered a woman over an hour and a half away, driven to Joe's and spent all night at my brother's homecoming party in the timeline they had.

Joe hung up. "That's at least a shred of good news." He sat down on a bar stool. "Let me have a scotch, will ya?"

I went behind the bar and poured him one and slid it across the counter to him.

"But they railroaded me before. They can do it again." I heard the panic in David's voice. "They'll pick me up for questioning. They'll want me for this."

"Look, this time you have real counsel," Joe said. "These fuckers are not going to do anything to you."

"If I may make a suggestion," Lewis said, "I think you should go to Billie's place, or Joe's. Call your father. Tell him not to answer the phone or door for the media. While you're lying low, Joe can negotiate a time and place for questioning. I'd invite you to stay with me, but I think my choice of artwork might make the cops wonder."

Joe nodded. "Good thinking. This is a temporary setback, man. But we got your back."

David looked at me. I nodded and smiled, trying to convey a confidence I didn't have. "It's temporary. You can crash on my couch until morning, which—" I looked at my watch "—is soon."

I grabbed his hand. "Come on…try to let Joe worry about it right now. He's a great lawyer."

David reluctantly nodded, and we left Quinn's Pub. In my car, I realized I'd never been alone with him. In prison, we had sat op-

posite a Plexiglas wall and talked on the phone.
We had sat opposite each other once or twice
across a table, but there were always people
around—or guards. Since his release, Lewis,
C.C. and Joe were always there when I saw
him. This was different.

"I didn't do it," he said as I shut the door and
started the car.

"It never entered my mind that you had."

I popped a CD in the stereo—my uncle had
a tricked-out stereo with killer speakers in the
Cadillac. I didn't want to hear what the news
breaks were saying.

"Who's this group?" he asked.

"Coldplay."

"Never heard of them. Never heard their music before. I like this song a lot."

I had a moment, an instant, in which I wanted
to say, *You're kidding? You never heard of
them?* But I realized the band became famous
in the vortex of time he had spent in prison. And
while I was sure boom boxes blared out in the
yard as men lifted weights, I knew it was more
likely rap or hip-hop than an English band with
lyrical sensibilities.

Movies were the same. The touchstones of
culture that I took for granted when I talked
with Lewis were gone when David was around.

Lewis and I had this weird habit of being able to recite memorized lines from every gorefest movie ever made. From Tarantino to old *Friday the 13th* movies, to *Dawn of the Dead,* we'd seen them all. Yet another reason Lewis never went on second dates. But with David, those references were useless.

I drove through the empty streets. The lights were synchronized, and we would go through ten greens before hitting a red. I tried to keep the conversation trivial, but my mind was spinning. I couldn't imagine how he was feeling. We arrived at my apartment and got out. I led the way and unlocked my door.

"It's not much, but it's home," I murmured.

"It's nice, Billie. Really nice." He walked over to the dining room table. "Is this where you work?"

"A lot of the time."

He wandered over to all my photos and immediately focused on my favorite. "Is this your mom?"

"Yeah."

"She was beautiful…. You look like her a little."

"I like to think so."

"When I was in prison, I used to think it would be easier on my parents if I had just died.

But then I thought about it. We had letters and visits. We had something, you know?"

"I have memories, but they're awfully faded. Mikey remembers more, but he doesn't like to talk about her. We go once a year to the cemetery, on Mother's Day. We bring flowers and we talk to her. But aside from that, we don't bring her up. It's a guy thing, I think. He bottles it up."

I went into the bedroom and brought out a pillow and a soft chenille blanket. "I'm sorry that my couch can be a little lumpy."

"Trust me. This place is a palace." He smiled at me. "I like picturing you now...you know, I'll be able to envision where you are when I e-mail you, or talk to you on the phone."

"Want a drink of water or anything? I'll crack the seal on a bottle of bourbon if you want and we can drink our way to sun-up. It's been a crazy night."

"I'm fine, really." He took a step toward me. "Billie...I really want to go on with my life. I want to live a life."

"I know."

He took another step toward me.

"Billie...can I kiss you?" he asked. "You can say no if you want. But I really want to kiss you."

I nodded.

"No pressure or anything—" he winked at

me, a little awkwardly "—but I haven't kissed a woman in ten years."

"I'd better make this good," I said huskily.

We reached each other in less than a second, I think, fiercely kissing. He held the nape of my neck, pulling me to him, into him, hungry for me. Our kissing had an urgency, and I just wanted to give in to it, to him, to whatever was this attraction between us.

I pulled off my top, and he pulled off his shirt. We didn't even move to the bedroom, just inched over to the couch, pulling the blanket around us, undressing and kissing.

"Billie," he whispered, as I straddled him. "Are you afraid of me?"

I stopped and held his face in my hands. "What?"

"Is there any part of you that's afraid of me?"

"No."

He now moved his hands to my face and kissed me, his hands very strong, his fingers stroking my cheeks. "Thank you. I just need this to be right."

We made love, right there in my living room. Afterward, I led him to my bedroom and we fell asleep as the sun was coming up. I knew that a media frenzy was building, but for a short while, shades drawn, blankets on top of us, the world was far away.

* * *

Joe called at oh-God-early the next morning: he had negotiated an agreement to have the police interview with David at Joe's home. A good plan, but when Joe came to pick him up around eleven that morning, I felt as though I was sending David to the executioner.

"Joe," I said, pulling my jacket tighter around me as we stood in the street. The January air was bitter and took my breath away. "He's going to be okay, right?"

"That's a relative thing."

David was waiting in the car with the heat on.

"What do you mean?"

"I mean there's no way they can arrest him— he's got an airtight alibi. We were all with him, he was seen in a public place. But any chance that guy had of getting a job, or moving on, just disappeared. Until we figure out what's going on, until the real killer is caught, his life is ruined as much as it was before."

I nodded.

"I guess I thought by freeing people, I'd be on the side of justice and that was enough. But it's not as simple as that," Joe said. He shrugged, helpless, and walked over to get into the car.

They pulled away, and I waved forlornly. Joe had just confirmed what I knew in my gut. I pulled out my cell phone and called Lewis.

"We need to catch the real killer," I said into the phone.

"I was afraid you'd say something like that."

"It's just like my mom's case. The police aren't going to solve it. They're looking to nail him, not find the truth. We have to do it."

"I know."

I'd expected more of an argument. But then he added, "C.C. already roped me into it."

"All right then, want to meet at my place at three?"

"See you then," he said wearily, and hung up.

I spent the next few hours researching. I decided the key to solving the case wasn't simply having DNA evidence exonerate David, although that was part of it. We would have to discover who was *behind* the crimes. The fragment of semen we'd found had been put into the database, but we wouldn't know about a match for a little while—if ever. What I had explained to C.C. after we first met remained true. If the real killer wasn't in the system, then it wouldn't matter that we had his DNA until the time came to prosecute an actual suspect. So I combed the Internet and waited for C.C. and Lewis.

When they arrived, I had a pot of coffee waiting, along with the roughest of theories. They seemed hesitant, awkward with each other, but I pretended not to notice.

"All right…let's shoot straight. Lewis, you're my best friend. C.C., you and Joe have become good friends. We've bonded over this case—and several bottles of wine, as well as margaritas—but before we throw our energies into what could be a dangerous investigation—and one that's completely renegade on our parts—we might as well lay our cards on the table. Does either of you have a fraction of doubt that he's completely innocent?"

I expected that Lewis might have—but he shook his head.

"You know him better than I do, Billie. But on science alone, I can believe him. Add your belief in him and C.C.'s faith in his innocence to the equation and any shadow of doubt is completely erased."

C.C. fiddled with the cross around her neck. "No doubt in my mind."

"Okay then. We have multiple ways of viewing this. When it became clear David was going to be freed, the Whitakers were all over CNN, *Larry King Live,* the *Today Show*, saying they still believe he's guilty no matter what the DNA shows. Harry Whitaker threatened me with a gun. It could be that Harry is behind discrediting David Falco."

C.C. nodded. "That's one theory."

"Displaced anger is a powerful emotion," Lewis offered.

"Problem with that theory is it required Harry to now kill an innocent woman. I don't think he's got it in him. This isn't a gun murder, either. It's a brutal killing. I don't see it, but we can't shut our minds to the possibility."

C.C. burst out, "Oh, God!" She abruptly stood up and ran from the table to the bathroom. Lewis and I could hear her muffled crying.

"Lewis?" I looked at him quizzically.

"She's really distraught over this, Billie. And I'm not helping any."

"What's going on between you two? Out with it."

"Nothing. I think we both recognize we…care about each other. Maybe even love each other. But there's nothing we can do about it. We haven't acted on it, so get that thought from your mind. But…we have muddled each other's lives up, that's for sure. She's ruined me for other women."

"Well, given your eccentricities, I don't think there were many realistic candidates."

He looked right at me. "I love her, Billie. As much as I love my tarantula, Quentin Tarantino movies and the New Orleans Saints. And jambalaya."

"Christ, it's serious." I patted his arm. "Go talk to her." I jerked my head toward the bathroom.

He nodded, but the door to the bathroom opened and C.C. emerged, clutching a tissue.

"Sorry, both of you. It's just that David was the gentlest prisoner I've ever met. This whole case is like Job. It feels Biblical to me, enormous. Overwhelming. I'll hold it together. Go on, Billie." She sat back down and Lewis clasped her hand and squeezed it.

"Okay. Theory number two points to a serial killer, even though we only have two victims to date. Now that David is out, perhaps the killer is angry. Perhaps the media attention reawakened this side of him in his mind. Maybe he's been dormant as the suicide king, but now he wants attention again. Who knows?"

"Serial killers don't 'retire,' Billie. So what has he been doing for the last few years?" Lewis asked.

"Killing."

"But…no calling card."

"No. A different calling card. Look, they put the supposed suicide king killer away. Threw away the key. So the real suicide king invents a different persona. Kills in a different way. Different calling card. Maybe he moves away and kills. Then Falco goes free. It pisses him off—so he decides to play mind games with the cops, with Falco, with the media. He's taunting us."

"I like that theory," C.C. said.

"You don't want to like that theory," I warned her.

"Why?"

Lewis looked over at her. "Because it will be like finding a needle in a haystack to catch him. If he's not in the system, the best profilers in the country would be hard-pressed to catch him. Serial killers are elusive until they make a stupid mistake and get caught, or, like BTK, they seemingly want to get caught."

"Oh." C.C.'s shoulders slumped.

"I have one final theory, if you two want to hear it."

"Shoot," said Lewis.

"We go back into Cammie's past. I keep going back to something David told me in the first interview I did with him in prison. He was trying to *help* her. She was screwed up in some way he didn't know or can't articulate. But she had something dark in her background. If we find out what that was, maybe we can figure out who killed her. Maybe whoever killed this woman in Atlantic City intended to frame David—so we can't discount that. But I think we should start with her. And also the card."

"The card?" C.C. asked.

"The suicide king *has* to mean something. It has to. Otherwise why leave it? I spent a few hours researching the history of playing cards. I didn't really turn up anything except some references to the French Revolution when it went from king high in the deck to aces high in deference to the antiroyalty sentiment."

"That seems like a dead end." Lewis looked upward at the ceiling, as if trying to connect imaginary dots in his mind.

"I thought so, too. So I kept digging…. It's a long shot, but there's a strip club named Stud's two towns down from where Cammie worked and David lived. It's a ten-minute ride. And guess what its logo is?"

Lewis stopped staring at the ceiling and looked at me. "The suicide king?"

I nodded. "Found them on the Internet pretty easy."

"So what do we do?" C.C. asked.

"We go and ask some questions. Could be a total dead end. Could be something."

"Well, what are we waiting for?" C.C. asked. Lewis and I stared at her.

"You can't go there," I said.

"Why not?"

"A nun going to a strip club? I think maybe you'd better stay home on this one, C.C." I said.

"Look," she replied. "I have all the parts those girls have. It's not like I'll see anything I haven't seen before. I mean they might be bigger and more silicone packed, but they're the same parts. I'm going."

"Well, it's not as simple as that, either. We're not cops or private eyes. So it won't be easy to get people to talk to us. And if there is some kind of connection, then it could be dangerous."

"So what do you suggest?" C.C. asked. "I'm in. You guys aren't cutting me out of this now."

I admired her spunk. "Well, I was thinking…what if Lewis acted like a big spender from New Orleans? He goes in separate. And me…I'll pretend I want to apply for a job."

"A job?" Lewis said, his voice rising. "You're how close to your Ph.D. and you want to apply for a job?"

"Give it a rest, Lewis. Don't worry. I'm not actually going to take my clothes off. Just going to inquire about a job there. So…tonight. Separate cars."

"And me?" C.C. asked.

"You go with me. Pretend like you're my friend, trying to give me moral support while I look for a job. Women always do things like that together. You'll have to borrow some of my clothes, though. We both have to look..." I searched for the right way to put it.

"Slutty," Lewis said, filling in the blank.

"Yeah, Sister Catherine Christine. Slutty."

Chapter 14

We checked in with Joe, who told us the questioning had been grueling but the police hadn't arrested David, just warned him to stick around.

"David's crashing here tonight," he told me. "He's spent."

"Okay…we're working on a few angles."

"What kind of angles?"

"Oh, you know, solving the suicide king murders."

"What?" His voice rose at least an octave.

"It's the only way he'll ever be free of this. We got him out of prison, but now we have to

free him from this following him around for the
rest of his life."

"You have any leads?"

"Not really. A hunch I want to check out."

"Is C.C. in on this?"

"Yes."

"You're not going to do anything dangerous
or crazy are you?"

"Me? Never. Talk to you tomorrow."

I hung up the phone and surveyed myself in
the full-length mirror on the back of my bedroom door. I was in full Slut Regalia, as Lewis
termed it. I was wearing skintight black leather pants—a gift from an old boyfriend. I had to
lie down on my bed and suck in my breath to
even get them zipped. On top, I wore a camisole in black lace. Ordinarily, I would have
worn a shirt over it—not tonight.

I stepped out of my room and looked at C.C.

"If anyone from the convent could see me
now," she said.

She looked stunning—if slutty. I had loaned
her a pair of stilettos—not my usual shoe
choice, either, but I had them left over from a
wedding outfit. She wore a black micromini,
black tights and a black sheer blouse—without the camisole under it, because I was wearing it. Between us, we had a whole unslutty

ensemble—but split up in two, we were tramps.

"I'm going to freeze."

"Yup. We'll wear our coats and blast the heat in the car. Come on."

Lewis was bemused. "I wish I had a camera, Billie. I'd love to post your photo on the bulletin board in the lab."

"Shut up."

"If only your old organic chemistry professors could see you now. Or perhaps your pals from Phi Beta Kappa."

Both C.C. and I had teased our hair big and Playboy-model-like, and we had on heavy makeup.

"Let's go get this over with."

C.C. looked at me. "You're sure *this* may help us find the killer?"

"No. Just a hunch, but it'll be okay, C.C."

She made the sign of the cross and whispered, "Forgive me," as we left my apartment with Lewis and went to our respective cars— Lewis in his, she and I in mine.

We drove the twenty minutes or so to Stud's. Neon blared it was a Gentleman's Club with Live Entertainment. The windows were painted over to prevent anyone from seeing inside— each window was a different face card. And front and center was an elaborate suicide king. We had agreed Lewis would go in first. If he wasn't out in under ten minutes, that meant the place was at least okay for C.C. and me to walk into.

C.C. and I sat in the car trying to keep warm.

"This seems like a real long shot," she whispered.

"I know. It's just a vague hope that it might lead us somewhere. Look, this case is nearly ten years old, right? Well, this club has been in existence since 1989. It was around when the murder took place."

"How do you know?"

"Look at the sign." I pointed.

She giggled. "Established in 1989. Good detective work, Billie."

"Anyway, that playing card meant something. If it was a serial killer, it meant something only in his tortured mind. If it was a warning or something specific to Cammie, then we should be able to find the connection somewhere. She had a dark secret, David said, and he felt some sort of sexual tension between her and the mystery man he says was there that night. This is the only suicide king reference I could find for several towns. It's worth a shot. But this is a really old trail, so we can't get our hopes up."

We waited ten minutes, and when Lewis didn't come out, we went inside. The bouncer at the door told us there was a twenty-dollar cover.

"We're here to apply for jobs," I said, batting my eyes.

"Go on in, then," he said. Tattoos covered every available inch of skin on his arms.

The interior of the club was very, very dark, with men scattered at tables near the stage or sitting at the bar. Some looked professional. Some a good deal rougher. Out of instinct maybe, C.C. grabbed my hand.

"Don't worry," I whispered. "We'll be okay. You're the one with a prison ministry. This will be easy."

A beautiful young woman, maybe eighteen, was dancing on the stage, gyrating against a pole. Her skin was shiny with sweat and baby oil, and her hair swept the floor each time she swooped down from the pole. Her muscles were toned, her belly flat. She had a belly button ring—a sparkling diamond—and rhinestone shoes five inches tall.

"She's awful flexible," I said.

"I couldn't even do that when I was her age," C.C. shot back.

We sat down at the bar. I ordered a bourbon,

and C.C. a glass of white wine. When she sipped it, she nearly spit it out.

"Oh, my God, but this is bad wine."

"Rude wine and breasts—what a combination," I said. "These places aren't known for their wine list, C.C."

I toyed with a matchbook and then leaned in to talk to the bartender over the pulsating music—a Moby song.

"I need to see the manager. I want to apply for a job."

I squeezed my breasts together with my upper arms. I'm a C-cup, but I was hoping to look more like a D.

"He's over there." The bartender motioned. "At that table."

"Thanks. What's his name?"

"Rick."

The manager wasn't what I expected at all. He had a very short haircut, almost executive-looking. He wore gray slacks, a black turtleneck and a simple chain with a medallion of some sort around his neck. He was clean shaven, and basically looked as if he would be at home in a boardroom. Meanwhile, the bouncer looked like a motorcycle gang member, and the bartender had a prison tattoo—or at least a homemade one—across his knuckles.

C.C. and I stood with our drinks and walked over to his table. I felt many pairs of eyes on me. I saw Lewis sitting with a pretty blonde in a peignoir set, drinking champagne, and he and I exchanged glances. I was grateful he was there.

"Excuse me, Rick?"

The manager looked up. "Yes? Can I help you?"

"Um, my name is Billie, and this is my friend Cathy, and…I was wondering if you have any openings for dancers."

"Sit down, ladies." He gestured to two seats at his table.

"Thanks." C.C. smiled wide.

Right away he noticed her gold band.

"You married?"

She looked down at her left hand. "This? No. Well, technically yes. But my divorce will be final in about three weeks. This keeps the real creepy ones away."

He took her hand in his. "I'm no creep," he said soothingly.

She blushed and took a sip of her wine.

"So, do you girls have any experience?"

I nodded.

"Where?"

"Place down in Florida. Back a few years ago. It's shut down now."

"You have a gimmick or anything?"

I shook my head, and purred, "When you see me dance, you'll know I don't need a gimmick."

He grinned. "I like your confidence. How about you?" He looked at C.C.

She shook her head. "I'm a cocktail waitress. I don't dance." She played with a curl in her hair, twisting it around her pinky.

"Too bad. If I sent you two out on some party calls, you'd make a fortune—the whole blonde-brunette thing. With the exception of twins, friends who are opposites, like you two, do best."

"You get a lot of party calls?" I asked.

"Hell, yeah. We can keep you as busy as you want to be. A lot of side money."

"Bachelor parties?" C.C. asked.

"Yeah. We book you for a grand each. You take $500. What you do on the side is up to you. We get a cut of everything."

Out of the corner of my eye, I could see Lewis waving a wad of singles at the dancer on stage. He was tucking dollars into her G-string.

"What I like," I said, "is this club has been around awhile. Club I used to work at, one day I show up, it's boarded up by the IRS or something."

Rick smiled at me. "We don't have problems like that. You'll always have a job."

"Let's say I started, what kind of shifts could I get?" I knew from a couple of girls who'd left stripping to be waitresses at Quinn's Pub as they got older, got boyfriends or settled down, that the lunch crowd was not as generous as the night crowd. No strippers wanted lunch.

"You'd work two days and two nights. Can't give you Friday or Saturday at first—you have to earn those. But stick around, show up on time, get a following, and trust me, you'll move into the big money slots."

"Great." I sipped my drink.

"Why don't you come back into my office for a few minutes? I can give you an application. I'd like to say yes, but I usually make you dance one shift before I hire. We can arrange a time."

"Okay."

He stood, and I followed him, telling C.C. I'd be right back. We walked through the club, my belly tingling with the bass that reverberated up through the floor. The dance floor–runway was illuminated from below. Mirrors on the ceiling and a dry-ice machine gave the room a dreamy quality.

Rick opened a door that read Office. Inside

was a classier take on the club. A dark purple velvet couch lined one wall, a wooden desk polished to a sheen dominated another wall. There were two computers side by side at a computer workstation—also in wood. A thick Oriental rug covered the floor. It was so thick my heels sank into it, and I almost tripped. When the door was shut, I could hear a muffled bass from the music, but it was quiet. My ears rang at the shift from the noise of the club to the relative quiet of this inner sanctum.

Rick opened a file cabinet drawer and pulled out an application. "Here you go, beautiful."

"Thanks."

"So what have you been doing the past few years, since you worked at the Florida club? You're not eighteen…" He winked at me. "But you're still drop-dead gorgeous."

"Well, I try to take care of myself. Most strippers seem to age in dog years."

"Clever."

"Clever? Or clever for a stripper?"

"Both. So…what have you been doing?"

"I was with a rich guy. Haven't worked. I thought he was the real deal. Yeah, right. I caught him in bed with not one but two hookers. We got in a fight, he gave me a black eye.

I took off with all the money I had, all the jewelry and clothes he gave me and my car."

I twirled around, looking at the photos on the wall—all strippers. "So who owns this place?"

"Why do you ask?"

I shrugged. "I like to be careful. Like I said, I don't want to end up coming here and finding it shut down."

"I said not to worry." His voice had a slight edge to it.

I walked closer to him. Now I had a clear look at the medallion around his neck. "Are you a cop?" I asked. I reached out and touched the medallion. It was a badge, with the number 135 on it.

"Used to be."

"When?"

"Twelve years ago. Got shot and left the force. Been here ever since…me and my partners."

"So *you* own this place?"

Without warning, he grabbed me and shoved me roughly up against the wall, causing my breath to leave me. I groaned.

"Are *you* a fucking cop?" He was twisting my arm, and I saw stars. I brought my knee up into his groin, and he doubled over. I moved away from him and he grabbed me, and then hauled off and slapped me across my face. I twisted out of his grasp on my wrist and ran for his desk and grabbed a letter opener.

I wheeled around and faced off with him. "Let me out," I said evenly. He had moved and was blocking the door. I waved the letter opener, which was solid metal and had quite a point on the end.

"Not until you tell me why you're asking so many questions."

"I told you. I want a place that's stable. Then I see you wearing a shield around your neck…I don't need to be near any cops. I don't like them, and I sure as hell don't want to work for them."

"Put the letter opener down."

"Move away from the door."

"You got fire, girl. I like a girl with fire. All right, listen, let's call a truce, okay?" He made a "calm-down" gesture with his hands. "Me and some pals own this place. We mind our own business, okay? I'm not a cop."

"Fine." I rubbed at the spot on my face where he hit me.

"Sorry about that. I just thought you might be undercover."

"No. I hate cops. I told you that."

"Still want the job?"

I clenched my jaw. How many desperate women had this guy abused and then turned around and hired? I mean, maybe it was just because he was suspicious I was a cop, but he sure as hell was quick to hit me!

"I'll think about it."

"I'm telling you, a girl like you could easily make four grand a week. Maybe more."

"Like I said, I'll think about it. Can I go now?"

He stepped aside, but I kept the letter opener out as I walked toward him. Once the door was ajar, I handed him the metal opener.

"See you around, beautiful."

"I bet you will," I muttered.

I went out to collect C.C. She saw the red mark on my face.

"Oh, Billie, what happened?"

"Let's just say that they didn't teach me in organic chemistry how to handle guys like him. Let's get going."

We collected our things, and left. On the way out the door, out of habit, I grabbed a matchbook from a giant fishbowl full of them. C.C. and I shivered as we walked across the parking lot. When we reached the car, I started it up and prayed for the heat to come on fast. It was so cold, my nipples physically hurt under the sheer camisole.

"So what happened?" C.C. asked, once we had warmed up again.

"I'm not sure. He started getting antsy when I asked him a couple of questions."

"So do you think this place had anything to do with the suicide king murders?"

"I don't know. Could just be a crooked strip club. We didn't have much of anything to go on to begin with." I played with the matchbook in my hand.

"Oh, my God…"

"What?"

I handed C.C. the matchbook.

Stud's had a "sister club" named Acey-Deucey's. Its logo was also a suicide king.

Its location?

Atlantic City, New Jersey. The location of the new murder.

Chapter 15

That Monday, Lewis and I had work, but we all agreed to meet at seven at Quinn's Pub to decide our next move. David had been named a "person of interest" by the media, though they also reported that he had an alibi. Still, I knew the police were circling like sharks in chum-infested water. We had to find out who killed Cammie—and the new victim, Liz—as soon as possible.

On Monday, during the day, I tested two samples of drugs. When cops make a bust, and they stumble on a cache of white powder, they don't have a case until we can tell them what that white powder is. Hell, you can't put someone in prison for trafficking in baby powder. So it's up to the lab to tell the police whether it's cocaine, heroin, crystal meth, or what. In bust number one, it was heroin—very pure. In bust number two, it was crack cocaine.

After work, I changed out of my lab coat and back into a thick black sweater over my jeans. Lewis and I decided to ride together, so I followed him to his house, left my car there, and we drove on to Quinn's.

"So you going to tell me what's going on with you and David?"

I shrugged.

"Come on, Billie."

"I don't know what it is. At first I told myself it was, I don't know, a reaction to his being in prison unjustly. Some sort of sympathetic response. But I can't say that anymore. It's something more than that."

"Seems both you and I have gotten ourselves into very inconvenient relationships."

"You can say that again."

"Well, then I suppose there's nothing left to do but clear David once and for all."

I glanced over at him. "Thanks, Lewis."

"And for the record, I like him much better

than Jack Flanagan and also better than the guy from the University of Pennsylvania you used to see on weekends. The one who hated jambalaya and didn't drink."

"I like David better, too."

We pulled up in front of Quinn's and went inside. My brother and Marybeth were having dinner before going to the movies. For a casual pub, Quinn's had amazingly good food, and I don't just tell people that because my uncle owns it. The chef in the kitchen was one of New York City's top four-star chefs—until he had a nervous breakdown from the pressure. He came into Quinn's on a bender three years ago and pretty much has never left. His nerves are calm, the food is awesome, he gets all the free beer he wants, and as a bonus, he's engaged to one of the barmaids.

I gave Mikey a kiss, stole a bite of his pasta and talked to him and Marybeth for a few minutes before heading to the back, where Joe, David and C.C. were already waiting.

Lewis and I sat down and helped ourselves to the pitcher of beer. David leaned over and kissed me on the cheek, which didn't even get an eyebrow raise from Joe, so I presumed David told him something was going on between us. Or maybe he hadn't had to. Maybe everyone else had seen it there before anyway.

"C.C. filled us in," Joe said. "I would have paid good money to see you both dressed like that, by the way. I smell blackmail."

C.C. playfully slugged him.

"So what do you think this club has to do with the two murders?"

"I'm not sure yet. We have what amounts to a hunch having to do with a playing card and a logo for a chain of strip clubs. We know this guy Rick is a former cop, that he's one of the owners, and he has partners. We need to find out more about his career in law enforcement, particularly when he was shot and left. Also, his partners. Anyone find the name of the second club interesting?"

"Acey-Deucey's? What does it mean?" David asked.

"Lewis? You play cards often enough with my dad. Want to enlighten them?"

"Maybe the partners play poker together. When you're playing with friends and you want to use wild cards in poker, you can pick acey-deucey, one-eyed jacks and…our friend the suicide king. Aces, twos, one-eyed jacks—only two of those in the deck—and the suicide king—only one of him. If the other club is named Acey-Deucey's, maybe it's named after their nicknames for each other during friendly games of stud, or maybe their favorite game. Who knows?"

Joe sipped his beer. "So we go sniffing around the Atlantic City murder and hope for some kind of connection to Cammie?"

"At this point," I said, "it's like throwing handfuls of wet spaghetti at a wall. In the end, we'll see what sticks. Maybe there's a connection. Maybe not. So we go to Atlantic City and investigate this, and then we do some more looking into Cammie's background—and we hope for an intersection."

"Okay. Lame and a long shot, but it's better than sitting around waiting for David to be arrested," Joe said.

Lewis leaned forward. "Joe…you know I'm your number-one fan."

"Ahh, flattery."

"I am, though. But I happen to be New Orleans born and bred. So tell me, how often do New Yorkers and Jersey-ites recognize you for being a former NFL player?"

"Rarely. Well, no, scratch that. I am recognized as a former NFL player a lot—just not by name. Sad to say it, but there's a stereotype. You're black and rich and you must be a rap-per. If you're tall, you play in the NBA. If you're built like a linebacker—" he grinned "—you must have been in the NFL."

"Perfect," said Lewis. "How'd you like to make a road trip to Atlantic City?"

"As long as I get to stay at the Trump Plaza and play some blackjack, I'm game."

Mikey came over to our table.

"So what are you guys? Like the Scooby Doo gang? Solving crimes?"

"Shut up, Mikey," I snapped.

"Can I be in your Scooby club, too?"

"The joys of having an older brother," I moaned. "Go away."

"Actually," Lewis said. "Maybe you can help us."

Mikey grabbed a chair from a nearby empty table and sat down. "I'm all ears."

Lewis said, "We're looking into the suicide king case—the old one. And the girl was a bartender at…what was the name of the place, David?"

"Finnegan's."

"Anyway, maybe you can go there—it's still in business. Ask around. Who knows what might turn up? But we want the street story, not what people said in interviews with the police. The police interviews made her seem like one step away from canonization. We know David's lawyer didn't dig at all, but there's reportedly something darker there. See what you can turn up amongst your 'legally challenged' acquaintances."

"Cool. For once I'm asking the questions instead of being questioned."

I smiled at his enthusiasm. My brother and I were very close. Growing up motherless children made us fierce defenders of each other.

"So can everyone go to Atlantic City on Friday?" I asked.

Joe took out his BlackBerry. "I take depositions in my office that morning, but if we left at five, I could do it. Want me to hire a limo? There's a guy I use."

I nodded. "In the meantime, I'll see what I can turn up on the latest victim."

David had been quiet the whole time we were talking. He sipped his beer, then said, "I want you all to know how much I appreciate this. Everyone please be careful. I couldn't live with this on my conscience if any of you got hurt."

I shook my head. "Don't worry. The suicide king killer is the one who should be afraid. He should be very afraid."

* * *

She was saying something to me.

My mother came into the bedroom of my dreams and tucked me in. In the crook of my arm, I held my Raggedy Ann doll. My mother kissed my forehead. Then she did an Eskimo kiss, rubbing our noses. She smelled like Ivory soap and faintly of lemons on her hands— she must have been washing dishes with the lemony detergent. She was crying.

"What's wrong, Mama?" I brushed her cheek, my hand still little-girl chubby, with dimples at the knuckles. I flicked my tongue in the space where my front teeth should have been. The tooth fairy had been visiting often.

"Nothing, Billie. You go to sleep. I need to do something. You're a good girl, right?"

I nodded solemnly.

"Then be a good girl and don't come out of your room until Daddy gets home later, okay? No matter what you hear. Promise me."

The hallway light half blinded me, streaming right into my eyes. I squinted at her. She was little more than shadows and darkness. Then, I saw a figure in the hall. I saw a man, but he was nothing more than a silhouette.

She saw him, too.

"Promise me, Billie," she said urgently.

"I promise."

"Good girl." She kissed me on the lips, then on each eyelid. "Go to sleep now."

Then my mother stood and exited the room, resignation and dignity in her posture.

The next sound I heard was a scream.

My own.

"Billie!" David was rousing me, shaking my shoulder. "Billie! Billie…wake up."

I woke and sat up in bed, the nape of my neck drenched in sweat though it was a cold night.

"You were having a nightmare, I think," he whispered. He was wearing boxers and a muscle T-shirt; his arms curled around me and he held me, my back to his chest.

"It's nothing," I whispered.

"Tell me."

"No…I don't want to. It's nothing."

"No…it is something. Tell me. Let me help you instead of you always helping me. It's important that I feel like…I give something to you."

Reluctantly, I exhaled. "Okay… It's always the same dream. My mother. The last time I saw her. Or think I saw her. The cops tried to tell me that my father coached me to say a man was in the house. At first they wanted him for her murder. But he didn't coach me. Still, the pressure of the way they interviewed me…it has my memory all muddled until I don't know what was told to me and what really happened."

I leaned against him. "I want your name cleared."

"Me, too." He kissed me. "God, I love your lips, your skin." He smelled my hair, nuzzled my ear. "Your scent. I love everything about you. It's like I'm still on sensory overload soaking you into me, Billie. And I don't think it'll ever wear off."

I kissed him back, pushing my nightmare out of my mind. It was as though we were racing against a killer. And I had felt that feeling before. With my mother. This time, I wanted to win.

Chapter 16

"One more Scooby Doo wisecrack and you're toast," I said to Michael as we waited for Joe's limo to arrive. C.C. and I had different disguises this time. We were dressed very expensively, as the girlfriends of an NFL star and his agent should dress. Lewis would be the agent, while David was going to play the part of college buddy in town for a good time. I was to be Joe's girlfriend. C.C. was Lewis's—which I noticed made Lewis happy. How horrible, though, to know that the pretend of draping his arm around her shoulders couldn't have been real, I mused.

C.C. wore her hair in a fancy updo. Marybeth was a hairdresser and she had us both looking as though we'd stepped out of a fancy salon when, in fact, we had been styled in my bedroom. I loaned C.C. my stiletto heels again, along with a black velvet dress—backless—and a beautiful black shawl inlaid with Austrian crystals that gave off little reflected beams of green and pink and twinkled when she walked.

I wore a black tuxedo outfit with a strapless bustier beneath the jacket. My hair was also up and long rhinestone earrings dangled from my ears.

Mike grinned. "You both look hot. No wise-cracks."

The limo pulled up about fifteen minutes later, and Joe called up with his cell.

"Wish us luck," I said to Marybeth and my brother.

"You're a Quinn. You got the luck of the Irish," Mike said. He never ceased to amaze me with his optimism. He never lost it—or rarely did. I guess that was what allowed him to bet on the Giants year after year.

C.C., Lewis and I all went downstairs and climbed into the back of the limo. The guys wore suits—Joe had taken David for one. We also put him in a pair of dark shades, and Joe took him to his barber, who clipped his hair short so he looked very little like the man whose face had been splashed on the news. We appeared, for all the world, like a wealthy group of old friends out on the town.

Despite, or maybe because of, the fact that we were going to try to solve a murder, we drank champagne and tried to relax on the way down to Atlantic City, keeping conversation light. We checked into rooms at the Trump—each of us had a change of clothes and toiletries in an overnight bag. Then we went on to Acey-Deucey's.

Acey-Deucey's was a classier establishment than Stud's. It had a gambling theme, and a prime rib buffet with hot and cold dishes. Tablecloths covered the tables, and Joe made it clear he was a former NFL player hell-bent on spending a lot of money. The stage was as nice as one on the Vegas strip, with lights and a sound system that was awesome. We were shown to a VIP table near the stage.

A Pamela Anderson look-alike was dancing, peeling off a skintight halter dress vaguely reminiscent of Marilyn Monroe.

"It's hard to know where to look," C.C. said, leaning close to me so I could hear her over the music.

"I know. Try focusing on her shoes."

Joe tossed around a lot of money and ordered top-shelf liquor. We hoped that his money act would bring over the owner or manager, and we could ask some questions.

"Let's go to the ladies' room," I said to C.C.

We told the guys we were going to powder our noses, and then went to the back of the strip club where the restrooms were. A glance down the hall showed me the location of the private party rooms. If a stripper could entice someone to pay for a private lap dance and party, she could earn hundreds or even thousands more.

Motioning to C.C., I drifted down the hall the other way to the manager's office, then farther on to the dressing rooms.

"What are you doing?" C.C. hissed.

"Pretending to be lost. Follow my lead."

I stepped into the dressing room. Women were in various stages of undress.

"Can I help you?" a beautiful redhead asked me. She was wearing only a thong and heels.

"I'm sorry.... We were looking for the ladies' room, and I definitely have had two cocktails too many," I giggled.

"Oh...go back the way you came. You'll see the ladies' room on the right."

"Thanks. Gosh, you are all so gorgeous. When my boyfriend wanted to take his old college buddy here, I was less than thrilled."

C.C. giggled. "Me, too. But you all are soo-oooooo talented." She emphasized *so* and acted a little tipsy. Hell, for a nun, she was a great actress.

"Glad you're liking it. We get a lot of women coming to the shows, believe it or not."

"Really?" I acted shocked. "Lesbians?"

"No…lots of couples. I get a lot of parties for couples. You should try it." She winked at me.

"Yeah…you might love it," another stripper added.

"You know," I whispered conspiratorially. "I had a friend, I'm talking years ago, who was a stripper. She was using the money for college…I took out student loans. She stripped. You know…you do what you gotta do. Then I met my boyfriend, and so now I don't have to worry about bills at all. But anyway, she would get some real creeps stalking her. Don't you worry? I read about a stripper being murdered and—"

The redhead burst into tears. "Lizzie."

"Hmm?" I acted surprised.

"Lizzie. You're talking about the suicide king killer?"

"Yeah, that one."

"Lizzie worked here for a while. She was murdered maybe a week ago."

"I'm so sorry," C.C. murmured.

"Did they catch the guy?"

"Not yet." The stripper bit her lip.

"Aren't you guys scared?"

I watched the women exchange looks with each other. Then the redhead put on a bright smile. "No. We're all right.... Anyway, you two better head back to your table before your boyfriends start to miss you."

"Yeah," I said to C.C. "Let's go. Good night, ladies. And good luck with your dancing."

"Thanks."

C.C. and I left the dressing room.

"That clinched it, C.C. There's a connection in these clubs."

"So now what?"

"Well, I'm not sure. We have to tie Cammie to the other club. And maybe we can find a match to the semen sample. We're not cops, and we're doing this outside law enforcement channels. We can't compel anyone to give samples. In fact, everything about us being here has to be under the radar."

C.C. and I turned the corner. I grabbed her arm fiercely.

"Don't."

"Don't what?"

"Don't move. Remember how we were hoping to bring the manager over?"

"Yeah."

"Well, he's there. The tall man leaning over talking to Joe. I think I'm going to be sick. It's my ex-boyfriend's old partner."

"What?"

"Yeah. The cop I broke up with at Christmas. His old pal. Look, he knows me. You go back to the table. Say that I suddenly felt ill and took a cab back to the hotel. And don't use my real name. Call me Angie."

"Okay." She turned to face me. "I'm scared."

"Don't be. We're going to be okay, C.C., but I just can't be recognized. I'll call Lewis's cell. And Joe's."

I dialed Lewis.

"It's me," I said when he answered. "Don't use my name. That guy you're sitting with? He's Jack's old partner, Marty O'Connor."

"Really?"

"Yes. And he knows me. I'm sending C.C. back. She's calling me Angie. She'll say I took ill and went back to the hotel. I'm leaving out the back way and will hail a cab. You guys take the limo and exit as soon as it doesn't look obvious."

"Okay."

"And we need to try to get a DNA sample from him. I know…it's not like you can ask him for one. But be thinking."

I dialed Joe and went through the same thing a few minutes later. I told him to hand the phone to David and pretend I was an old buddy of both of theirs. I didn't want any of the guy's to question C.C. and blow our story.

David was very flustered. "Let me come meet you for cocktails, pal," he said into the phone.

"No. We don't want to risk him being suspicious at all. All of you leave in like a half hour."

I closed my phone. C.C. was on her way back to the table, tottering on heels. The red-head was out on stage. I moved over to a back exit and pushed on the door. I was outside in the cold and hurriedly cut through the parking lot. It smelled like snow. I walked and soon was near the fence that surrounded the parking lot, when I heard two men talking. I heard the name Lizzie and ducked next to a car, creeping forward to try to eavesdrop.

"You think they did it?"

"I'm not paid to think about that."

"Stupid bitch. Fell for a john."

"In this biz, it pays to stay unattached. It's all

smoke and mirrors, my man. Smoke and mirrors."

"And tits and ass."

They both laughed.

And at that moment, my phone rang.

"Shit," I muttered under my breath. I should have put the thing on vibrate. I turned it off.

"What was that?" I heard one of them say.

"Someone's over there."

"Fuck...go get whoever it is."

I looked around in panic. I had a huge parking lot to cross. No one else was around. It was cold. I was in heels. And then for good measure, an icy sleet started to fall.

I scrambled toward the next car, staying low, trying to avoid being seen.

"Over there! Grab her!"

"Shit!" I looked down at my shoes and up at the sky. Wear the heels in the slick sleet, or go barefoot and deal with the agony of my stocking feet on cold ice? I decided on the latter, abandoning my shoes and making a run for it.

They were maybe twenty feet away—and both were in shoes, not to mention being nearly the size of Joe Franklin.

I slipped and slid, and tried to keep my balance. They were having an easier time of it, but were by no means unaffected by the ice. The wind shifted and suddenly it started coming down harder. The sleet hit my skin like cold, sharp blades. I shivered even as I sweated from concentrating and running.

Suddenly, I lost my footing, flying across the parking lot concrete and smashing face-first into the hubcap of a Lincoln Navigator.

"Shit!" I blurted out as I saw stars for a second.

"She's over here," one of the goons shouted.

I rolled over. My tux jacket was ruined, that was for sure. Scrambling to my feet, I tried to run, each step leaving me with my arms flailing. The two guys were flailing, too, and slipping, but they were definitely gaining on me.

My mind flashed, in an instant, to the Murphy brothers and numerous bar fights at Quinn's Pub. My father and Mikey never lost a fight—and not, my father told me, because either of them was a better fighter or better built or anything like that. They won because they were *smarter*. Both of them could think on their feet—and improvise. A Quinn family trait.

Think, Billie.

I looked around. Still no one was in the parking lot. It was up to me to get free of these guys or, I presumed, end up tossed off a pier into the cold Atlantic Ocean.

Then I saw them. My weapons of choice.

Sliding and slipping, I raced for a long line of metal garbage cans—heavy-duty. I pulled off one top and flung it like a Frisbee. It hit the bigger of the two guys right in the knees and he yelped.

I flung a second one at the other guy. And missed. And now he was plenty pissed.

My face was swelling where I'd hit the Lincoln Navigator. My cheek was puffy and starting to swell into my line of vision. That was it! The Lincoln.

I scanned the parking lot and noticed it was packed with expensive cars—big spenders. And big spenders with big, fancy cars have car alarms.

I started racing from car to car, pulling on handles and slamming the trunks with my fists. Car alarm after car alarm came on.

If there's one thing those who are operating outside the law hate, it's alarms, attention and cops. I knew that because my brother broke out in a cold sweat every time he saw a cop cruiser, even if he hadn't been doing anything wrong.

I watched as the two of them froze. They looked at me, looked around the lot, judged the mess I'd just created, and then turned on their heels and ran back for the club.

I stepped gingerly to the fence, clung to it for balance and walked to the exit. Out on the sidewalk, what looked like a group of guys from a bachelor party were climbing out of two cabs. I slid into one, hoping to avoid being noticed for my lack of shoes. And my smashed-up face.

Avoiding eye contact in the rearview mirror with the driver, I said, "The Trump."

"You got it."

The cabbie pulled away. I felt in my jacket pocket for my cell phone. I searched the inside jacket pocket for money and found a twenty: one reason I loved the tuxedo was not having to carry a purse. I dialed Lewis.

"Hello?"

"Lewis, it's me. Listen…I just got chased, and I'm pretty beaten up."

"What? Are you all right? Where are you?"

"On my way back to the hotel. Have you all left yet?"

"We're in the limo."

"Great. I'll be in my room. I'll tell you all about it when you get there."

I leaned my head back against the cab's seat, shut my phone and felt my face with my fingers. I closed my eyes and tried to wrap my mind around Marty being at that club.

I had never liked Marty. Jack said a lot of

spouses and significant others of cops were threatened by partners. As a team, partners shared in the adrenaline highs and depressing lows of a dangerous, life-threatening job. It was the job, or, the way Jack put it, The Job, that bound partners together.

I understood the bond. Jack was wrong. I wasn't threatened at all. I was grateful, in fact, that before I met Jack, when his daughter died and he went through his divorce, it was Marty who made sure Jack didn't swallow a bullet. But once Jack got over the immediate intense grief, once I met him, I wasn't so sure Marty was a good influence on Jack. For one thing, even as Jack struggled to stop drinking so much, Marty was the first one to suggest hitting the local tavern for a drink.

I wasn't sure how this strange assortment of coincidences and connections was tied to the suicide king killer. I only knew we were getting closer to the truth—which meant we were in more danger than ever before.

Chapter 17

I walked through the glamorous lobby as fast as my now agonizingly painful feet would carry me. I kept my face down, and skulked into an empty elevator car, which carried me up to the twelfth floor. I was sharing a room with C.C., Lewis and David were sharing, and Joe, the big spender, was in the penthouse suite.

I got off the elevator, grateful for the carpeting, and entered my room with my key card. I immediately dead-bolted my door and went into the bathroom and flicked on the light.

My face was a red, shiny mess. A nice black

eye was developing, my cheek was swollen, my mascara made me look like a raccoon, and I had scraped my forehead pretty badly. My chin also was the recipient of a nice red welt.

I rinsed my face with warm water, then washed my red, scraped feet with hot water. I undressed completely, went to my overnight bag and pulled out my sweats and the big sweatshirt I'd brought to sleep in. I was so grateful for the warmth. I pulled on a pair of thick athletic socks, sat down on the bed, and gently massaged my feet to try to warm them more.

A few minutes later, Lewis and the gang arrived. I stood and went to the door and peered through the peephole to be sure. Then I opened the door and let them in.

"Oh, Billie," Lewis said, actually wincing at the sight of me. David came over and hugged me. Then he stepped back, winced himself, and kissed my lips ever so gently.

"Let's get you to the hospital," Lewis said.

"No!" I was adamant. "No…I'll be okay."

"What happened?" Joe asked.

I went though the entire story from the minute I'd spotted Marty.

"I'm going to have to turn Ripper loose on these guys," Lewis said, trying to make me smile.

"Trust me. These guys would stomp Ripper. Hey, David...did Marty seem like he recognized you from any of the coverage?"

David shook his head. "Nah. He was sucking up to Joe big-time."

"Good."

We all sat down on the two beds. I leaned my head on David's shoulder.

"So when do we go to the police?" C.C. asked.

"Not yet," I said. "Not yet."

"Why?"

"C.C....we're talking about two cops owning strip clubs—one of whom maybe had a dancer who was killed by the suicide king. It's not like they're the good guys—I mean, yes, some cops are. But in this case, we may be talking about rogue cops. And all we have are hunches—when the police are thinking David is their best suspect. We have proof of nothing."

"So now what?"

"We go back to that club and find out who that redhead is."

"The stripper we were talking to?"

"Yeah," I nodded. "We get her to talk to us somehow, and we find out why Lizzie was killed. She knew something."

"Aren't the police already doing that?" C.C. asked.

"Maybe. Maybe not. Either way, they think she was killed by a random serial killer—or David. No one thinks there's a connection beyond the killer, so nobody's looking for one."

"I'm not following. They didn't cover this kind of stuff in my religion classes," C.C. said, half smiling.

"Okay…years ago, the suicide king killed a girl. He killed again last week. The connection? The police think it's David. Or if not David then some random killer. The connection, aside from the killer? The cops think nothing. It's random. Both girls were in the wrong place at the wrong time. Only now we know that's not true."

"But they *were* in the wrong place at the wrong time," she said.

I nodded. "But that's not the *reason* for their deaths. Follow? There's some other connection, but no one's looking for a reason other than randomness. We find the reason, we find the killer."

"I'm in this until the endgame. We get whoever did this," Joe said.

Lewis looked at my face, then he looked at C.C. "In New Orleans," he said, with his usual drawl making it sound like N'awlins, "we don't back down from a fight. Let's get the bastards. Sorry, C.C."

"I told you, Lewis...sometimes even the Lord himself understands the value of a few choice words."

"Well, guys, I love you all, but I'm falling asleep as I'm sitting here," I said.

"You sure you don't want to go to the hospital," Lewis said.

"Positive. Go on and play some slots, Lewis." I smiled as best I could with my puffy face.

"I'm hitting the tables," Joe said. "Help me relax."

David said, "I'm not, I better get some sleep myself."

Lewis, though, got a devilish look in his eyes. "Well, a few hands of blackjack never hurt a man."

I looked at him. "Don't come crying to me when you run through all your spending money."

The guys left, and it was just C.C. and me. I went to brush my teeth, then sat down on my bed. She was changing into her pajamas.

"C.C.?"

"Hmm?" She slipped a nightgown over her head.

"Can I ask you something?"

She smiled. "I've been waiting. I knew sooner or later you and I were going to have to lay our cards on the table—we're in Atlantic City, so the metaphor seems appropriate."

I smiled—which hurt my cheek. I pulled down the covers and slid under the sheets and blankets.

"Okay… You're the first nun I ever met. So you get to answer all my nun questions."

She laughed.

"So why'd you become a nun? I mean, you're beautiful, funny…you're nothing like what I expect a nun to be."

"My grandmother was a deeply religious woman. My mother was the polar opposite. Still is. My mother married for money—she makes no secret of that. And my parents divorced when I was young…they've both since remarried several times, to other people. I had everything money could buy—except the peace that surpasses all understanding. And that I got at church when my grandmother visited."

"How did your mother turn out so different from her own mother?"

C.C. shrugged. "She just has a love of *things.* Cars, clothes…and she doesn't scratch the surface or look too deeply. But with my grandmother, I would see this beautiful example of faith. And I knew, from the time I was a little girl, that I wanted that. I wanted that faith, that peace."

"Do you have any brothers or sisters?"

"No. I've had, I think, fifteen stepsiblings over time—by different spouses of my parents. But no blood siblings."

"Your mother must have had a cow when you said you were going to be a nun."

"She blamed it all on her mother. They still don't speak. I don't hold out much hope for a reconciliation."

"And you're really celibate?"

"Yes. I'm really celibate."

"C.C., I can't even imagine. I mean, I've never thought of sex as something casual. Sex, for me, has always meant something. I've gone months and months without meeting someone I thought was worthwhile enough. But give it up entirely?"

"That's just one part of my life."

"And Lewis?"

"Honestly, I don't know. I love him. I love him in the most profound way, with all of my heart and soul. And I love him in *that* way. I mean, being a nun doesn't take away the capacity to fall in love. You just choose to forsake that life for the love you have with God. But…I don't know. I've often wondered if I could have my faith and have a family and a different life. Or if, indeed, this was my destiny. Whatever happens, Lewis will teach me something deep about myself. I don't mean to hurt him. I'm as confused as he is, I suppose."

"Lewis is my best friend," I said. I rolled over on my side and looked at C.C. in the other queen-size bed. "He's the smartest man I've ever known, the most eccentric and the most loyal. I just want you to know that he loves you…and if you love him, too, that's all I need to know. What you two figure out is your own business."

C.C. looked at me. "Thanks, Billie. I pray each day for God to let me know his plans for me. And as soon as I know, I plan on letting Lewis know."

"Could you pray to God for David, too?"

"Of course. I pray for him daily. I pray for you, for Joe, for all the men in my prison ministry. Do you pray for David?"

"I don't pray."

"Why not?"

"I don't know. I suppose I feel like God's too busy to listen to me. I guess the conversation feels pretty one-sided. And I have so many questions."

"You'd be surprised. He answers. It just may not be the answer you want. But if you're still, if you're open to it, he will speak to you, Billie."

"But what if more women die before we can catch the suicide king? What if David is framed? What if we do all this and we can't save him? Where is God in that?"

"I choose to think God is there in the new friendships we have. If the worst happens and David goes back to prison, he'll have the four of us fighting forever to free him. He won't be alone."

I punched at my pillow and rolled onto my back.

"Maybe."

I tried to fall asleep, but I tossed and turned all night. I waited for the whisper of God, but instead all I heard were the sounds of drunken gamblers returning to their rooms, and the soft drone of the heat coming through the vents in our room.

Chapter 18

"Hello?" Lewis said into the phone. "Listen...I just got into town, and last time I was here, I met the most beautiful redhead at your club....

"Yes, Ginger. Yes...that was her name. Yes, well, I was hoping to perhaps have dinner with her while I was in town and was wondering if I might be able to leave a message or get her number or...

"Um, yes, sure."

Lewis's eyes widened. I tried to lean in closer to him to hear the other end of the conversation.

"Yes...um, sure. Three o'clock then."

He hung up the phone. C.C. and I, and David and Lewis had checked out of our rooms, and we were all in the penthouse, which Joe had taken for a second night so we would have it for the day.

"Well?" I demanded.

"She's coming here on an out call. She's a hooker."

"The plot thickens," I said. "Like Rick told me, these cops own places fronting prostitution."

"So maybe the killer was an angry john," David said.

"Maybe. Do you think Cammie was a hooker? Did she give off that vibe?" I asked.

"I don't know. I mean, I've spent ten years of my life reliving a night over and over again, with a half-fuzzy memory of a woman I didn't know too well. I have no idea what kind of vibe she gave off. It was too long ago."

"It's okay," I soothed. I thought of the nights I lay awake trying to remember my mother's voice, or the smell of her perfume, and only ended up with the faintest whispers. Were those the whispers of God?

"So what do we do when she gets here?" C.C. asked.

"Lewis," I said, "you greet her. Agree on the price and so on. Get her to sit there," I gestured toward a sofa that was the farthest from the door. "Then C.C. and I will come out. We'll try to talk to her. Those girls were scared."

"Sounds like a plan," Joe said.

"David, you stay in the other room," Lewis said. "We don't need the man whose face is synonymous with the murders to be question-ing her. It could spook her if she recognizes you."

David nodded.

Joe ordered room service lunch and the five of us played cards for a couple of hours. Out of deference to C.C., who said she felt a little guilty being in Atlantic City, let alone waiting for a hooker, we played rummy instead of pok-er.

At two forty-five, David hid in the other room, Joe hid in the bathroom with C.C. and me, and Lewis poured himself a straight bour-bon from the minibar to steady his nerves.

"I never paid for it before…and frankly, do-ing it in the guise of hunting for a murderer is giving me the creeps."

"This from a man with a pet tarantula," Joe teased.

In our hiding spot, I cracked the bathroom

door a hair, and when a knock at the door came, I peeked out. It was her all right, but she was dressed beautifully. My guess is she didn't want to tangle with security at the hotel and had to look like a guest.

I heard murmurs as she and Lewis discussed price. He offered her a drink, and she went to sit down on the couch. That was our signal. C.C. and I stepped out from the bathroom.

"What the fuck!" she said, standing up.

"Wait." I held up my hands. "We just want to talk."

"Look…I'm not into any weird shit. You want the rough stuff or whatever, you call Serenity."

"No…it's not that," C.C. said softly, sadly. "Honest. We just want to talk."

"About what? You're the two women from last night. And what happened to your face?"

I reached up a hand involuntarily to touch my bruised cheek and chin. "My guess is maybe the same thing that happened to Lizzie."

"What the hell would you know about what happened to Lizzie?"

"We were hoping you might help us," Lewis said. "We don't want to scare you or alarm you."

I took a few steps toward her, slowly.

"Please, Ginger. Please help us to find out what happened to your friend."

She looked me in the eyes. "Mind if I have a cigarette?"

"No."

She rummaged around in her bag, and then suddenly emerged with a can of Mace pepper spray.

"Easy," Lewis said. "We don't want to hurt you. You don't want to hurt Billie."

"You're right. I don't. But I will unless you crazy people let me out of here."

I saw her finger was on the button that at any minute could release toxic chemicals right into my eyes. This had *so* not gone as I intended.

I looked at Ginger and said, "Maybe we can help you."

"Help me? What makes you think I need help?"

C.C., Lewis and I were frozen in our places. I was taking a risk trying to get her to talk to me, but I figured I didn't have a lot to lose. I had to get her to put down the pepper spray. I knew I'd survive it. I also know I'd be in agony—and I'd had enough pain the night before.

"I don't know. Something about when we were talking about Liz…you looked scared."

"Someone gets his freak on by killing her

and they haven't caught him? You'd be scared, too."

"It was more than that, Ginger. I mean, you can mace me, but it was more than that and hurting me won't change anything."

"I'm C.C."

Out of the corner of my eye, I watched C.C. approach her. Ginger's finger twitched on the release button on the pepper spray.

"And this is Billie," C.C. said. "I'm a nun. My whole life is dedicated to helping people. I'd like to help you."

"A nun?" Despite the tense situation, Ginger smiled. "A friggin' nun? You're kidding me, right?"

C.C. shook her head. "Now, maybe you aren't scared and don't need help. But I don't know any little girls who say 'I want to be a prostitute when I grow up.' Lives change, events happen, and we all follow different paths. If you need help, we will give it. We can keep you safe. We can get you away from here. Far away. Help you start somewhere fresh."

"You're really a nun?" Ginger asked, this time softer and more fragile.

C.C. nodded.

"Shit." Ginger put down the hand with the pepper spray in it. Lewis and I still stayed where we were. "A nun? What are you two? FBI agents?"

"No. Just a couple of people caught up in this case. I'm a criminalist from the crime lab in Bloomsbury. Lewis is my boss. We want to figure out what really happened to Liz."

"Good luck," Ginger said derisively, less scared but no less defensive. "Listen...you can't beat these guys."

"Why? Just because they're cops?" I said.

She shook her head. "Because they're hunters. They're serious fucking psycho hunters."

C.C. moved toward her. When Ginger didn't whip her pepper spray arm up, C.C. moved closer and closer, then wrapped an arm around her. "Come sit down," she urged.

I marveled at how gentle C.C. was, and yet how brilliantly she zeroed in on a way to get through to Ginger. She had a real gift.

"What do you mean by hunters?"

Ginger sat on the couch, and now I could see that she was visibly trembling. "I gotta go. And I gotta have money with me when I go back."

"We'll take care of that," Lewis said. "But maybe you don't have to go back."

"Look...these guys, the girls who work this side line for them...we all have something to lose. We're handpicked."

C.C. looked at me and I opened my eyes wide and gave a slight shrug to my shoulders to say I didn't understand.

"Handpicked?" C.C. asked.

"Yeah. Brothers who have a record that maybe these guys made go away, sisters headed for prison, parents in trouble, children that might grow up without you. Lately, a lot of Eastern European girls with no passports and all kinds of problems. They find out your weakness, make you an offer, and then you're in until they get tired of you."

"So what's your story?" I asked.

"How old do you think I am?"

I looked at her closely. "Twenty-eight?"

"Good guess. And I have a little girl. She was born deaf. And she goes to a fancy boarding school for kids who can't hear. I get to see her weekends. She has everything she needs. And if I don't behave, then…she enters the foster care system. I had one positive urine test at the club. No judge is going to give a kid to a mother with a record and a job as a stripper who tested positive for cocaine, which I did with the fucking owner, by the way. At school my girl is so happy. She signs, and she can type on the computer. She writes me an e-mail every day. She thinks I work as a concierge."

I realized my mouth had gone completely dry. I had no saliva, and I could barely swallow. What sort of men were these guys? Blackmail, abuse...murder.

Suddenly, Joe walked out from the bathroom.

"Wait a minute. He's the NFL guy from last night. What's going on?" Ginger asked, recoiling.

C.C. wrapped her arm tighter around Ginger's shoulders. "He's my dear friend. He's okay."

"Look," Joe said. "Your child is not going to enter foster care. You're not going back to that club. And your daughter is going to get the schooling she needs. You got that?"

"I don't have any money...I don't have anything but what I came here with. I was so in debt when I first started at the club. I couldn't make ends meet. I couldn't afford private care for her. I knew a few signs. That was it. Now we can talk—you know...signing. But I got nothing."

"That's enough," C.C. said, "if you have your dignity."

Ginger snorted. "Dignity. That doesn't go too far in this town."

Joe came over to the sitting area and said, "I

will personally pay for your daughter's boarding school. You tell me more about your daughter."

Ginger, broken a second before, now seemed to glow a little. "She's the most beautiful little girl you ever saw. Her name's Harper. After Harper Lee."

I arched an eyebrow at Lewis. Ginger saw me.

"Just 'cause I strip doesn't mean I don't try to better myself. I read."

Joe smiled at her. "Want a drink?"

She nodded. "Vodka on the rocks, if you have it."

Joe went to the next room and got David and then poured her a drink.

"Who's this one now?" Ginger asked.

"Another friend," C.C. said. "Go on…about Harper."

"Well…when I had her, I had a boyfriend. We were planning on getting married. I was twenty-one. He was twenty-three. Worked in construction. I was a secretary. The pregnancy was really hard. I had really bad morning sickness—well, morning, noon and night sickness—the whole nine months. I couldn't work. So before she even got here, we were pretty desperate. In a lot of debt. But she came out all adorable with these red curls. Cutest baby you ever saw."

"Do you have a picture?" Joe asked.

She nodded. She put the pepper spray back into her purse and pulled out a wallet. She showed us a picture of a beautiful little girl.

"Here's her baby picture," Ginger said, passing the wallet around.

"Very pretty," I murmured.

"Anyway, when she was, I don't know, maybe six or seven months old, she didn't babble. She wouldn't turn her head when you talked to her. She didn't turn her head if I put music on. A couple months after that we found out for sure she was deaf. My boyfriend left. I tried to go on welfare. But she needed early intervention. Some was available through the state. But not much. Not what she needed. So…I started dancing. But with paying a babysitter, and a therapist for Harper, and rent, and all the rest of it, I was barely making ends meet. So when they came to me to offer me a spot as a call girl, I jumped at the chance."

She looked around at us. "You ask any mother, if it's between her child and herself, she'll always put the child first."

"Of course she would." Joe said. "Who made you this offer?"

"Marty. And Charlie."

"Who's Charlie?"

The other partner. One is Acey, the other Deucey. Charlie is a cop. A detective. And he's the real bastard. Marty sometimes seems a little sympathetic. But not Charlie."

"Where is Harper's school?" Joe asked.

"Bergen County… Look, um, who *are* you guys?"

"Ever hear of the Justice Foundation?" Joe asked.

She shook her head, and then he told her about David's case and the new murder.

"We don't think Lizzie was a random victim. We think she was killed because of her connection to these cops."

Ginger nodded. "Look…you all seem like you really want to do the right thing, but I need to go back. I have Harper to think of."

Joe came closer and knelt down in front of her. "You think I'm bullshitting you? We're going to your place now, getting a few things. Then we're going to Harper's school and taking her out of it—just until this thing is settled. I'm taking the two of you someplace safe. We're shutting down these clubs, and we're figuring out which of these bastards is a murderer."

"How?"

"DNA…'cause as my friend Billie tells it, we all have a personal bar code."

Ginger looked from Joe to C.C. to me, to Lewis, and finally David. "I've never been so terrified in my whole life. I don't even know you people."

"Sometimes," C.C. said, "you have to make a leap of faith."

Chapter 19

By seven o'clock, we were on the road in the limo, heading toward northern New Jersey. Lewis had suggested getting Harper in the morning, but Ginger told us that when she didn't show for her night dance shift, they might suspect something. So we arrived on the grounds of the Addison School around nine-thirty. Ginger signed the sleepy little girl out, saying there was a death in the family. As soon as Harper was in the limo, head on Ginger's lap, she was fast asleep again. From the Addison School we traveled to Joe's house, which had room enough for all of us. We needed to regroup.

"It's just about time for us to go to the cops," Joe said. "We need to find one we can trust."

I thought of Jack. Things had ended badly, but surely he wouldn't want his ex-partner enslaving women into prostitution.

I went upstairs to shower and change, borrowing a clean sweatshirt and socks from Joe. The sweatshirt was huge on me, but it was warm—and I was tired. I laid my belongings out on the bed. The tux was ruined. Then I looked at my cell phone. I must have put it on vibrate at some point, but it flashed on its digital screen "5 new messages." I hadn't heard it ring.

Four calls were "urgent" from Mikey. One from Jack, of all people.

I called Mikey.

"Where are you?" he asked.

"Joe's house."

"Stay put. I'm coming to you."

"Can't you tell me over the phone?"

"No. Give me Joe's address."

After I hung up, I climbed in the shower. It was hot and felt great. Ginger and Harper were tucked in down at the end of the hall. I had rarely witnessed so sweet a scene as when Ginger talked to her daughter in sign language. Lewis was downstairs having a drink with Joe and David and C.C.

I dialed Jack's cell phone.

"Jack?" I said cautiously. "It's me."

"Baby…what have you gotten yourself into?"

"Nothing," I said.

"Billie…you're in deep trouble. You need to stick with what you do at the lab and leave solving crimes to the police."

"I don't think so, Jack. The police are the problem here. They don't want to solve the crime. They want a fall guy."

"Look, you just have no idea what you're messing with here."

"Wait a minute," I whispered. "How do you know I'm involved?"

"Surveillance tapes. The club's got eyes all over the place. Reviewed the tapes after an incident with a woman in the parking lot. Funny…the woman in the parking lot looked a *lot* like my old girlfriend, Marty said. I looked at the tapes and guess what? It *was* my old girlfriend."

"Jack, Marty's into some really nasty stuff."

"Billie—" his voice was urgent, heavy with emotion "—I still love you. I've been wrecked since you've been out of my life. Wrecked. I'm trying my hardest to make sure you're safe, but if you don't listen to me, it's out of my hands."

"Jack…" I warned, "just stand clear, because when this house of cards falls, I don't care who I take with it."

"Is that a threat?"

"No, Jack…it's someone who once loved you and knows what you've been through, trying to get you to see that covering for these guys is a mistake. Be careful, Jack."

"Be safe."

I disconnected my cell phone. At least I knew we were most definitely on the right track. I went downstairs to wait for Mikey and told the others what had transpired on the phone.

"I knew I didn't like that guy," Lewis said.

"Lewis," I reprimanded him. "At least he's trying to warn us. We need solid proof, but I'd say we're pretty damn close."

Suddenly, I had a thought. I hurriedly dialed Mikey. "Where are you?" I asked him.

"Just getting ready to get on the turnpike."

"Can you go to my apartment and get something for me?"

"Sure." My brother and father both had keys to my place—so did Lewis.

"You know where I have all those pictures in the wall unit?"

"Yeah."

"I think on the right-hand side, way at the back, is this eight by ten taken at a police department picnic two years ago. When I was with Jack. We had played softball and took this massive group shot. Can you get that and bring it?"

"Sure thing. You okay?"

"Yeah. Will be more okay when we're done with this mess. Can you grab me some clothes, too?"

"No problem. See you in a little while."

I closed my phone and looked at David. "I have this photo from the police department. It has a shot of Marty—who you met at the club. And also just about every other cop from that precinct. Maybe, if there's a connection to Cammie, one of those guys is the person who showed up that night. Then—" I turned to look at Joe "—we'd have an eyewitness, the dirty club, Ginger's ordeal, and we can go to the police with the whole damn thing, wash our hands of it and let them get the bad guys."

"Well, for all of us to be safe, we have to go to the police or the FBI. We now have a little girl sleeping upstairs, her terrified mother, and you were attacked in Atlantic City. I think enough is enough. Time to bring in the big guns," Joe said. "Outside the local cops. Has to be someone we trust."

Lewis started pacing. "I have a friend in the FBI. Agent down in New Orleans. After the hurricane, they moved him to Atlanta."

"You trust him?" Joe asked.

"Like a brother. I was actually a college professor until someone…very important to me turned up a floater in the bayou. I damn near lost my mind. She'd been tortured, along with a half dozen other women. This FBI agent, Tommy Two Trees, he interviewed me. Asked questions about my sanity. Hard to believe but I was a tad off center."

I looked at C.C. Her eyes were moist, and she was studying him as he spoke.

"Tommy is a big bear of a man. Interesting guy. Half black, half Native American in a city that takes people's racial origins seriously. Always looked at askew, like people don't know if he's black or foreign. Drinks Bloody Marys so hot it'd scorch the average person. I call him T-cubed. You know, three Ts in his name. Anyway, T-cubed took me out drinking one night. Let me wail at the moon over my first love. When the night was over, I somehow had made a decision to leave academia, which is how I met you folks. Tommy and I have been friends ever since."

"This isn't his jurisdiction," Joe said.

"Doesn't matter. I can call him right now and short of a nuclear bomb being detonated in the middle of Atlanta, he'll be here, no questions asked. I don't like to burn through too many favors, but I'd say it's time to ask for his help."

"Call him," I said firmly, handing him my cell phone.

Lewis nodded. He flipped the phone open and dialed this guy's number.

"Tommy?"

We watched as Lewis paced and talked. "I'm in a bit of trouble. Billie and I—yes, that mobster's daughter I work with." He covered the mouthpiece. "Sorry, Billie."

Lifting his hand again, he spoke. "Seems we may be close to solving the suicide king murder, and it's most definitely not the man who went to prison for it. Oh? You saw me on CNN." Lewis looked pleased. "Well…the thing is, now it's gotten decidedly deadly. I can't tell you all of it over the phone, but looks like some officers of the law are actually the villains. And I need someone I can trust."

Lewis nodded as Tommy spoke. Then Lewis picked up the conversation again. "Yes, yes, I still have that tarantula…. Well, I don't understand a man your size fearing a hairy spider. Well, sure, but…but…all right, then, Billie will spider-sit while you're up here. See you tomorrow." Lewis closed my phone.

"You have that much pull with an FBI agent?" Joe asked.

"There is my charm."

I rolled my eyes.

"What?" C.C. asked.

"I'm a man of many talents, but that's a story for a different evening."

About a half hour later, Mikey's car pulled into Joe's driveway. I went to the front door and opened it, throwing my arms around my big brother when he got to the door. He gave me a huge hug in return, and we held each other a few moments. Usually, it's the other way around with us—he's in trouble up to his eyeballs and I'm scrambling to make bail.

"Dad wants to know if you want the O'Malley twins to come keep watch."

"After what happened to Tommy Salami, I'm not dragging anyone else into this. Come on in."

"What happened to your face?"

"Slammed into a hubcap. Long story."

Mikey followed me into Joe's den, where everyone was waiting.

"Want a drink?" Joe asked.

"Yeah…a beer, if you have one."

Joe nodded. He had a wet bar, so he opened the small stainless steel refrigerator and handed my brother a cold bottle of Michelob. Mikey twisted off the cap and took a big swig.

"All right…I asked around. Word on the street is Cammie Whitaker was working as a call girl."

"What?" I sank down into a chair.

"Yeah. Only it's a lot more complicated. Seems she was the golden child. Cheerleader, A-student. Bartended to pay for school, but she was nothing like your typical call girl."

"How come the police never turned up her past?" C.C. asked.

"Seems no one looked. They nabbed David quick, and her family was anxious to keep certain things out of the media."

"They knew?" I asked. That sort of explained Harry's near breakdown.

"Not in so many words. But they knew she was running with a crowd they didn't like. And they didn't like the fact that she was always with older guys. A lot older. And rumor has it she was being groomed. You know, a girl like that…educated, beautiful, she can command a high price."

"But why would she go along with it? What would make a girl who had everything throw it all away?" C.C. asked.

"A married boyfriend. Her self-esteem was in the toilet."

"Wow," I said. "Mikey, that explains so much. And it links her, almost, to the new murder. Do you have my picture?"

"Oh, yeah. Nearly forgot. I left it in the car."

Mikey went out to retrieve my picture. I felt pretty pleased with how things were coming together. "Once Lewis's friend comes, then we should be able to wrap this up."

"Amen to that," Joe said.

Mikey came back in with the picture in the frame and set it down flat on the coffee table.

"David…come look at this. See if any of these cops was the man at her apartment that night. So far, we have Marty and Rick, and a cop named Charlie. I'm not sure who he is, but the FBI will figure that out. So one of them might be the actual suicide king. The DNA match. You saw Marty, so we know it's not him…take a look here." I slid the photo toward him.

"Can you turn up that light?" David asked.

Lewis turned the dimmer switch until it was pretty bright in the room.

"Found him." David's voice was confident. Resolute.

"That was fast," I said. We all clustered around the photo, peering over his shoulder so we could see the man he pointed to.

"That guy there."

"Oh, my God," Lewis said.

"What?" C.C. asked.

Lewis looked at me, as tears streamed down my face.

"That's Jack Flanagan," he whispered. "That's Billie's ex-boyfriend."

Chapter 20

A half a box of tissues later, I had stopped crying. Now I was mad. At Jack…but also at myself.

"How can you blame yourself?" David asked. He sat next to me, rubbing my back.

"Because I have an IQ of 148 and graduated valedictorian, and I should have figured it out. The clues were all there."

"Where? What? Did he keep a big ice pick under the bed like Sharon Stone in *Basic Instinct?*" Lewis said. "I've met the man a dozen times, I never picked up that he had a screw loose other than his drinking."

"No…look. The poker-playing foursome. He played poker with some cop buddies. So now it all makes sense. Acey, Deucey, Suicide King…and One-Eyed Jack. That's Jack. My Jack. My ex-Jack. And I bet if we go online now, we'll find a strip club called One-Eyed Jack, with the same logo."

"Let's go to my office," Joe said.

We followed him in a group and stood behind him as he logged on.

"Nice computer," I said, momentarily distracted. His was state-of-the-art with an enormous flat screen that put my home computer to shame.

Joe went to Google and did some searches. Sure enough, One-Eyed Jack's was a strip club in Hackensack.

"He was the married cop," I whispered. "He once told me that his marriage was dead long before his daughter got sick. That he had these dark things in his past. Was trying to put them behind him. He was Cammie's married lover."

Mikey let out a low whistle. "Man…this is so fucked up. I hate messing with cops. You guys better be damn sure you're right because if not, with a name like Quinn, Billie, you're going to be risking pissing off every cop between Ft. Lee and the Jersey Shore."

"You and Dad have taken care of that nicely," I said. "Besides, I'm more worried about these particular four cops than anything else. They have a lot to lose."

"Can you prove all of this?" Mikey asked.

"Close enough. We called the FBI."

Then a thought flew into my mind.

"Oh, my God! Oh, God…I *can* prove it. Beyond a shadow of a doubt. Beyond anything."

"How?" David asked.

"Jack's toothbrush."

"What?" C.C. asked.

"Jack's toothbrush. After we broke up, I threw his things into a cardboard box. Figured one of these days we'd have closure. You know, meet, have dinner, talk about what happened between us…I'd give him his things, he'd give me mine. He still has a sweater of mine and my favorite bathrobe. Figured we'd be all adult about it. Anyway, that toothbrush has his DNA on it. We match that to the DNA from Cammie…and gentlemen and Sister Catherine, we have ourselves a murderer."

"How soon can we test it?" Joe asked.

"Tonight. At the lab."

"What are we waiting for?" C.C. asked.

"Lewis and I are the only ones who can go in the lab. You all wait here."

"I'm coming," Mikey said. "I brought a piece."

"A piece?" Lewis asked. "You brought a gun?"

"Now, Lewis," Mikey said. "There's no use talking me out of it. The bad guys always use real bullets, so the good guys need them, too."

"I wasn't going to talk you out of it," Lewis drawled. "I was just going to ask if you were a good shot."

"Lewis, if my sister is in danger, trust me…no one will be a better shot than me."

So I found myself at eleven-thirty at night, driving through New Jersey with Lewis and Mikey. First I got Jack's toothbrush. Then we headed to the lab.

I thought by the time we got there that Mikey would have driven Lewis stark raving mad. When Mikey is worried, he's a motormouth. So the entire time we were driving around, he proceeded to tell Lewis everything from the baseball batting averages of the current Yankees lineup—though spring training was months away—to his current legal predicament using his Al Pacino in *Scarface* impersonation, to the time he found my training bra and soaked it in water and froze it.

Lewis was silent. Finally, he said, "It's a wonder, Michael, that you don't confess immediately when picked up by the police. Do you ever shut up?"

"Oh, trust me, Lewis. When the *police* are involved, I exercise my right to remain silent."

"Remarkable," Lewis said sarcastically.

Soon, the lab loomed in the distance, its sign lit up with bright spotlights. We parked the car and entered the building and left Mikey with the security guard—I was taking no chances leaving him in a car alone after the Tommy Salami incident. Then Lewis and I headed to the lab, swiping our cards and putting our thumbs up to the scanner.

I loved the lab when it was empty. I liked getting lost in a microscopic world. From a quantum physics perspective, I subscribed to string theory, and I loved knowing that the world is only our perception of it. Beneath the surface, hidden from the human eye, was a universe alive and always moving, particles and creatures, crystals and DNA that could reveal a hidden truth. The smallest trace could tell you a story, tell you whispers of crimes past.

Lewis and I worked together.

"Your brother…he's quite bright, isn't he?"

"Mikey? Yeah. Why do you say that, though? I could tell he was making you nuts. He likes to talk."

"You think?" Lewis let out a half laugh. "I could tell he was smart. Those batting averages...he rattled them off like they were nothing. Details...great memory he has."

"Yeah. He was always like that when it had to do with gambling, sports, whatever."

"So what made him use his brain for...certain illicit activities, and you use your brain to become a criminalist?"

"I guess it was sexism in a way. My father groomed him to follow in his footsteps, and both of them groomed me to stay out of trouble and get an education. I was never allowed to date any of Mikey's friends. I mean, not that the guys would try."

"Oh, come on...they must have."

"You kidding me? My brother would have broken their legs—literally—if a single one of them even dared to ask me out. I went to my prom with my *cousin*."

"What? You're beautiful!"

"Thanks, Lewis. But no one would ask me out. My second cousin on my father's side—he was from Manhattan, so no one knew he was my cousin. Still, I felt like the biggest loser in the world."

"How do you think Mikey feels about David?"

"I don't know. As I got older, as long as the guy was a real gentleman, they were at least slightly less pit-bullish. But then I was so involved in my work that they started to worry. What if I *never* got married? So then they started bugging me to find someone, to settle down."

"Can't win, eh?"

"Not hardly."

We worked through the night, and near dawn we were ready to look at the film and see if Jack's DNA matched the semen left on Cammie Whitaker.

Lewis grabbed my hand before I could look. "Now, Billie...whatever the evidence says, we're going to get through this."

"If he did it, Lewis, how could I, of all people, have loved a killer?"

"There was always something wounded about Jack, and you responded to that. I think that makes you special. So forgive yourself. Before we even look, forgive yourself."

"Okay."

"Don't okay me. Look me in the eyes."

I did. "Okay, Lewis."

"You'll always be the love of my life, Billie. As a friend, as a sister to me."

"I know. Now shut up with the mushy stuff. Let's see what the film says."

We looked, holding hands—encased in latex gloves—down at the strands of DNA, the lines and dots of blackness exposed on the film. There was Jack's DNA. There was the DNA left on Cammie Whitaker's panties.

They were a perfect match.

Chapter 21

Lewis and I closed up the lab and went out to the security guard station, where Mikey was waiting, fast asleep.

"Mikey," I said, nudging him awake. "We can go now."

"Well?" he asked, stretching and standing up, rubbing his face.

"It's a match."

"Come here, baby sis," he said, enveloping me in his arms, rock hard from prison workouts to combat the boredom.

I leaned my face against his chest and took

a few deep breaths. There was only one person on earth who understood what it meant to lose my mom as a child, and that was Mikey. My father lost a wife, a lover, a friend...but Mikey was left motherless, just like me. He had guarded me fiercely when we were still children, and though we were both grown, he was still my protector.

"Mikey's here for you, baby sis. I'll rip that guy to shreds."

I looked up at him, a single stray tear trickling down my face. "Don't. This once we're letting the authorities handle things. Jack's not worth it. He's not worth the tiniest of parole violations. So don't. You let Lewis and his FBI friend handle it."

Mikey clenched and unclenched his jaw, finally agreeing.

The three of us went out to Mikey's car and headed back to Joe's. Everyone was asleep—except for Joe, who was in his office working furiously, his fingers flying across his computer keyboard.

He turned around when we entered the room and looked right at me. I gave a single nod.

"You okay?" Joe asked me.

"As okay as I can be right now."

"You look beat...why don't you go catch some z's. I'm working on a contract for one of my NFL guys—I actually have to make money sometimes to support this pro bono stuff."

"Tough thing, earning a living," Lewis said.

"Yeah," added Mikey.

I shot him a look. "Michael Anthony Quinn, you've never worked an honest day in your life."

"I know. Still a tough thing earning a living."

I shook my head. "You going back home? Marybeth will be worried."

"I'm not leaving your side until Jack is in cuffs."

I knew it was futile to argue. "All right, then. I'm going up to bed."

I trudged up the stairs to the guest room with my things in it. David was sleeping on top of the blankets, fully clothed. I watched him sleep, his breaths deep and even. His face reminded me of a statue my grandmother once had of a Raphaelite painting, very classic. Around his eyes were a couple of tiny crow's-feet, but he was remarkably not worn down by prison. For the hundredth time, I wondered how he had survived the living nightmare of being there unjustly. I knew I would never look at DNA the same again after this case. I would always know that the science of my job could free the wrongfully accused or imprison the truly evil, and now that I had gone through both ends of that spectrum with people I cared about, science would be more alive than ever.

I lay down next to David and snuggled into the crook of his arm, resting my head on his chest. He stirred.

"Hey, gorgeous. I was waiting up for you, but I guess sleep got the better of me."

He rolled onto his side and kissed me. "You okay?"

"Yeah. The DNA was a match. That cloud of suspicion over your head? It just evaporated."

"I wish it could have evaporated without you going through so much." He stroked my face. "I decided what I want to do with my life. You know how you and C.C. said I should take some time, absorb what I'd been through, then figure it out?"

"Yeah." I touched his cheeks, which were prickly with stubble. "I remember."

"Well, I'm going to take that book deal and use the money to pay for law school. He doesn't know it yet, but someday I'm going to work for Joe."

"That's a fabulous goal."

"And I plan on learning how to make you smile. I'll practice every day. Promise."

He kissed me on the lips, and though I was exhausted, I squeezed against him and kissed him back, pouring my grief over Jack and my fears into the moment.

We made love, and then, truly falling asleep with my eyes open, I murmured something about being so tired and passed out.

Lewis knocked on the guest room door.

"Billie? David? Tommy Two Trees is here. I need y'all to come downstairs."

I was in a deep sleep, the kind in which you drool and lose all track of night and day. I woke up and had no idea what day it was, what time it was, or even *where* I was.

Eventually, events started coming back to me—like the DNA match. I shook my head to wake up more fully and said toward the door, "Be down in a little bit. Ten minutes."

I climbed out of bed after waking David with a kiss and a little hug. I went into the bathroom and washed and dressed, pulling my hair into a ponytail for simplicity. David came in a minute or two later and started the shower.

"I'm going downstairs," I told him. "Come down when you're ready, okay?"

He nodded, stripping out of his boxers and stepping into the shower. Since prison, he said his lone vice was very long, very hot showers.

I went downstairs. Lewis and Tommy Two

Trees were sitting in the den with Joe, C.C., Mikey, Ginger and Harper. Lewis and Tommy Two Trees stood. I was in awe of how *huge* the FBI agent was. His legs were like two tree trunks, and I wondered if that was at the root of his name.

"T-cubed, may I present the woman responsible for this prematurely gray hair of mine— Billie Quinn."

I stuck out my hand, and Agent Two Trees took it in his mitt of a hand, and then leaned down and gave a little half bow. "Pleased to meet you, Billie. Any woman that can give Lewis gray hair is a woman I'd like to buy a drink for."

"Why, thank you." I smiled at him. He stood about six feet six, and his skin was copper colored. He had a shaved head, which only made his ebony eyes stand out more—like shiny black pieces of mica. He wore a suit in dark blue, with a tie—and a pocket handkerchief. I hadn't seen one of those in years. In a nod to his Native American heritage, he wore a bear claw on a black leather cord around his neck. The claw was enormous. Rather like Two Trees himself.

"Lewis has filled me in…along with Ginger, Joe and C.C. You have quite a team assembled.

Don't know as I have *agents* as hell-bent on un-covering the truth as you bunch."

"Thanks."

"Oh, it's only half a compliment. The other half would like to stick you all in handcuffs and throw away the key. You don't go off with some crazy idea on a serial killer or multiple murderer, no badge, no backup. You could have ended up dead."

"But instead we caught the guy who did it," C.C. said.

"Well…we need to tie up a few loose ends first."

"Like what?" Joe asked.

"Like," T-cubed said, "we don't know who did this for sure."

"What?" I snapped. "We busted our butts to get the DNA evidence. The DNA says who did it."

"Maybe…maybe not." Tommy Two Trees turned to me. "Lewis told me you were…a spit-fire. If I *had* hair I'm sure you'd be making it gray by now."

"So what do you mean *maybe?*"

T-cubed walked over to the coffee table and removed several glossy books from its surface, along with a stone statue of a Buddha head. Then he lifted the coffee table, made of heavy dark wood, himself, with no help, as if it were made of toothpicks.

"Lie down," he commanded me.

"What?"

"Lie down." He pointed to a spot on the floor. I shrugged and obliged.

"Ginger," he said to our newfound friend. "You take the little girl upstairs. We're going to be reenacting a murder."

Ginger nodded and signed to Harper. The two of them left the room. As they went up the stairs, David came down, his hair wet and slick from the shower.

T-cubed crossed·the room in three strides. "Tommy Two Trees. Pleased to meet you."

"David Falco."

"I'd like to express my…sorrow to you for your unfortunate incarceration. You know, we in law enforcement like to think we're all on the same side, all doing the right thing."

David nodded. Then he looked at me lying on the floor.

"Indulge me," T-cubed said.

Lewis came over to me and stared down. "Pretend you're dead."

"No," T-cubed said. "Pretend you're alive for the moment…. Lewis, you be Jack Flanagan. Joe, you're going to be bad cop #2, Mike is bad cop #3, and David, you can be bad cop #4."

Lewis said, "We did this reenactment thing in New Orleans."

"Lewis has a way of thinking like the criminal mind," T-cubed added.

"If I'm Jack Flanagan, I make love with this girl…and then what? Skewer her brain with a knife?" Lewis said. "Doesn't make sense. I rape her and skewer her brain with a knife? When we're dating? Is it power?"

T-cubed nodded. "Keep going, Lewis. Stream of consciousness. Let it go…talk aloud." He stood off to the side as Lewis began to pace and think and talk aloud.

"I go to her house and we make love. I wear a condom, because I'm married and I don't want to get her pregnant." Lewis spun around. "We argue, and I…hand me that pen, will you, C.C.?"

C.C. handed him a Cross pen from the rolltop desk.

"We argue," Lewis continued. "And I try to stab her. Resist, Billie…"

He knelt at my side and pretended to come at me with the "lethal" Cross pen. I wrestled with his arm.

Lewis looked up at Tommy Two Trees. "Impossible. She would fight like mad, there'd be stab wounds on her hands—there were none in the M.E. report. There would also be blood all over the place. Spatter."

Joe said, "None of that in the report, either."

"Exactly," said T-cubed.

"Bad cops—" Lewis gestured "—you all hold Billie down. Billie—" he looked me in the eyes "—fight as hard as you can. As if your life depended on it."

Mike grabbed one arm, Lewis another, Joe a leg and David the other leg. Lewis said to them, "Hold her down as hard and as strong as you can."

They each applied pressure to me. I felt myself panic. I knew it was all a reenactment, that I wasn't really going to be hurt, but instinct took over. I started fighting them as hard as I could. I kicked my legs and thrashed my head from side to side. I lifted my body off the ground, flinging my pelvis forward, straining and struggling.

As I struggled, I started sweating and my panic grew. I tried to kick my legs. I moved my head from side to side. I fought until I literally had no fight left. Slowly, I resigned myself to not escaping them. My muscles twitched and ached.

At that moment, Lewis came at me with the Cross pen. That reignited the panic and I wouldn't hold still. After a few minutes, Tommy Two Trees said, "Stop, let her go."

We were all out of breath.

"Lewis? Your take?" T-cubed asked.

"Even with all four holding her, she would be screaming and fighting. I don't see it. Too messy, too…frankly, sick. One of them might be sociopathic, but four cops all sociopathic enough to do this to a woman? I don't see it. I can see them committing gang rape or even harming a woman, but this was a bizarre crime."

His friend nodded. "Ideas?"

Lewis stood. I lay there for a minute, gathering my thoughts. Suddenly I sat up.

"Special K."

"What?" C.C. asked. "The cereal?"

"No," my brother said. "She means the drug."

"I don't follow," Joe said.

"Special K is made from a horse tranquilizer. I bet you one of those cops was in narcotics. Given enough Special K, someone's going to be virtually paralyzed. Wouldn't take nearly as much to stick a knife in them."

"They may not have run the right tox screen

on Cammie way back when," T-cubed said. "But we can run it on the woman killed in Atlantic City."

"Doesn't solve which of those fuckers really did it," Joe said. "If we're going to fry one of those cops, I'd like to be sure we fry the right one."

"We haul all four in and see what shakes down," T-cubed said, rocking back on his heels.

"No," I said. "They'll all flip on each other and create reasonable doubt. You'll get them on the prostitution charges, maybe. But you won't nail them for the big crimes. Let me confront Jack and wear a wire."

"No way."

"Come on," I begged. "I don't want them to walk."

"Look…it's out of the question. I'll talk to the head of the field office here. Don't worry, these four aren't going anywhere. Now…did someone say breakfast was available?"

Lewis smiled. "I did inform Joe of your prodigious appetite. Seems that's something the two of you have in common."

"Let's go," Joe said. "I had stuff delivered."

We all made our way into Joe's immense kitchen. I could have turned several cartwheels in it and not hit a thing. The long table, with seating for ten, was set up with two dozen or so bagels with four different kinds of cream cheese, a fruit platter, fresh pots of coffee, juice, champagne and doughnuts and pastries.

My mouth watered, but still, in the pit of my stomach, I was mad. I just didn't want these four cops to have killed two women, ruined lives, locked David away, and then what? Serve time on lesser charges? I wanted whoever killed Cammie and Liz to get what was coming to him.

I tried to shrug it off, but it was hard. Eventually we all ate, although I'm not sure what I would call what Joe and Tommy Two Trees did. *Eating* seems like such an insignificant term for it. They devoured an amount of food that made me sick just watching.

"Mr. Two Trees?" C.C. said. "What do you like to be called? T-cubed? Tommy? Thomas?"

"Tommy is fine."

"Which is why I call him T-cubed," Lewis piped up. "Like to get right in his craw."

"You?" I mocked. "Lewis…you're usually so mannered."

"Lewis is a character in his own right," Tommy said.

"Tell us," C.C. said. "Tell us something we don't know about our Lewis." Her eyes sparkled.

"Hmm," Tommy said, taking a bite of a bagel—which meant he bit off half. He chewed and swallowed. "You all know about his tarantula. His blood spatter pictures. But do you know about his brain collection?"

I looked at Lewis, who said, drolly, "I tried to keep a few things about my private life secret. So…I have a few brains."

"What?" Mikey asked.

Tommy nodded. "We used to go to this bar in a rough area of New Orleans. There was this shop, specialized in the 'black arts.' We went in there one time, and there were these jars lined up, filled with formaldehyde, and like six different kinds of brains—monkey, dog, cat…. Lewis bought the whole damn collection. You should have seen the looks we got walking through the French Quarter that night."

"Brains," I said. "Why does that not surprise me? And where *are* these brains? I've never noticed them before."

"They're in my pantry. Next to the spice jars. I just haven't found a good place to display them."

I shook my head. "Lewis, sometimes…" Before I could finish my sentence, my cell phone rang.

"Hello?"

"Billie?"

"Jack?"

"Billie…I told you to keep out of this. I told you to just keep out. Now you've really made a mess of things."

"*I've* made a mess of things? Jack…do you have any idea how much trouble you're in? Look…Jack…" I was staring at Lewis, my eyes saying, *holy shit, what do I say?*

"Billie…I did try to warn you."

Something about Jack's tone of voice made me uncomfortable.

"When playing poker, it's best to be holding all the cards."

"What do you mean?"

"It means I want the DNA sample from Cammie destroyed. I didn't kill her, and I'm not going to the executioner."

"I can't do that, Jack."

"Hold on."

There was the sound of muffled voices. And then a voice way too familiar, sounding sad, anxious. "Billie? I'm sorry, honey—"

Then Jack's voice. "I'm playing hardball. Don't call the police or the feds or he's a dead man."

Then silence. He had hung up on me.

I folded my phone as everyone looked at me expectantly.

I looked up at Mikey, my voice catching.

"They have Daddy."

Chapter 22

"What?" Mikey grabbed the nearest thing, which happened to be a coffee mug, and hurled it against a wall.

"Mikey…" I tried to soothe him, but my brother wasn't about to be calmed. He bolted from the room. I looked at Joe. "I'm so sorry…"

"Don't worry, Billie. Go after him."

I ran to the next room, where my brother was pounding his forehead with his hands, saying, "No, no, no, no, no…" over and over again.

"Mikey," I whispered. "Mikey, don't." I took

his fists into my hands and stopped him. "Mikey, love, it's okay. We've got the FBI here. We'll get Daddy. We will, honey."

He looked at me. "If they harm a hair on his head, Billie…"

"They won't. If they do, they'd have the wrath of the police, the FBI, and more importantly, the Quinns, on them."

"Why would they do something like that?"

"I don't think they know about Tommy Two Trees. We haven't gone to the cops yet. So for all they know, they can negotiate the DNA sample and go home free."

"Home free? We have Ginger. We have the body of that woman in Atlantic City. They have prostitutes working at their clubs."

"All of which means exactly what I said before."

"What?"

"That they can create reasonable doubt. Without the DNA from Cammie, you basically have four corrupt cops who own strip clubs. I don't think that's illegal in and of itself. And you have the word of a stripper turned hooker—tell me how fast that would get destroyed in court. You're talking walking on the big stuff and going down for a few things that, even if they're convicted, wouldn't amount to much time."

"Shit, Billie. I'm calling in the boys."

The boys meant the Quinns. All of them in the business of whatever it was the Quinns did a shade or two under the radar.

"Keep the boys out of this. Mikey…this time, let's work *with* law enforcement, not against it. Tommy Two Trees in there seems like a good guy. Someone we can trust. Okay? Come on."

"We lost Mommy. If they hurt Dad, I'll kill them with my bare hands."

I stared at my brother and for maybe the first time I saw how fragile he was under the surface. He was the motherless boy who had protected his little sister and had to grow up way too fast.

"I know, Mikey. But they won't hurt him. Come on."

We went back into the kitchen, where C.C. was picking up the last pieces of the broken coffee mug.

"I'm sorry," Mikey said sheepishly.

Joe put up his hands. "Hey, man, no problem. We got ourselves a situation, and sometimes, in a situation, you gotta lose it for a few minutes. We're cool."

"Cool," Mikey said in return.

We both sat down, and Tommy asked me, "All right. Repeat exactly what he said, as near as you can remember it."

I repeated the conversation.

"I have to call the local field office."

"Don't," Mikey said. "Don't. Let's handle it ourselves."

"We can't," Tommy replied. He looked right at me. "But I swear to you and your brother, we will get your father and nail these mother-effing bastards to the wall. You see this?" He held up the bear claw.

"Yeah," I said softly.

"I went hunting with my father and grandfather and killed a bear the summer I turned twelve. It made me a man, and it made me a warrior. And I'm telling you, warriors don't go down. We don't. We have a power that the bad guys can't see. It's almost mystical. You're a warrior, Billie. We're going to get them."

David came over to me. "We'll get your dad back. Look at what you and Joe and C.C. and Lewis were able to do. On your own. Put some resources behind you guys and you're unstoppable."

I looked up at Mikey. He nodded.

"All right. In the meantime, what do I do if he calls again?"

"Keep him on the line, but he's slick. They're cops. I mean, they're the slickest of them all. They know the score on what we can do with wiretaps and so on. Basically, you're going to have to think on your feet and don't for a second let on that you have an FBI agent here."

My cell phone rang again.

"Jack?"

"Meet me, with the DNA film and the original underwear from the crime scene, at our place. I'll leave a boat for you at the landing. Seven o'clock. Sharp. Don't fuck with me."

"Jack..."

"You and those Justice Foundation people should have left him in there. Kept out of it."

He disconnected.

I looked at everyone. "We're screwed. He wants me to arrive with the DNA film and the panties—alone—at our place."

"Where's that?" Tommy asked.

"A small spit of an island in the middle of Greenwood Lake. We used to picnic there. No way for any agents to hide. No way to get to it but by rowboat or small motorboat. Isolated. It's winter. No tree cover. He's smart. He knows I'll be alone."

I sank my head into my hands.

"Now Wilhelmina," Lewis said. "You really think I'm going to let one alcoholic cop get the better of me and my six brains?"

I smiled despite my predicament. But I

didn't see how we were going to win. Mikey came over to me and kissed the top of my head.

"Look at me, Billie."

I glanced up at him.

"How many times do I got to tell you? You should never fuck with the Quinns. Jack Flanagan and those cops are gonna wish they had never been born."

Chapter 23

We basically had eight hours to get an entire plan together. First, Lewis and I replicated the DNA samples again—and then, for safekeeping, again. What Jack and his cop pals didn't understand was that DNA can have a life of its own.

Blood spatter on a wall, painted over, or in a car trunk's carpet that's been steam cleaned, will still glow under the light once Luminol is applied. And a fragment of DNA can be duplicated over and over again.

Then, we went to Kmart and bought a pair of underwear in the same size and a similar pattern as Cammie's. I highly doubted Jack and his pals would remember her damn underwear. We took the panties back to Joe's and washed them five times. I added a few teaspoons of bleach to fade them. They didn't quite look ten years old, but I sealed them in a gallon Ziploc baggie and hoped Jack would be fooled.

In the meantime, the FBI had put some scuba divers on the shore of the lake, hidden in a boathouse. The waters were icy, and even with dive suits they couldn't stay in long, but they would be sent into the water once I started toward the island.

Also out of sight would be helicopters with sharpshooters with infrared devices. They would be ready to fly over the island at a moment's notice. According to Tommy, if my father was with Jack, they'd try to grab them both before they even got to the island.

"And if he doesn't have my dad with him?"

"It's all a careful and delicate dance. We've got surveillance on all four clubs. You'll be wearing a wire."

Mikey didn't like any of this. "You're not sending my sister to meet with this fucking psycho. He stuck a *knife* in a girl's head. In her *head*. Do you realize how fucked up that is?"

Tommy walked over to Mikey—we were in Joe's den, which was now a mini command central—and put his hands on Mikey's shoulders. "I do. I could curl your hair with the stories of shit I've seen in my line of work. But the truth is, she's your sister and Lewis's friend. So no matter what I say, none of you all is going to relax. I can only tell you that this guy will have to kill me to get to her. I will lay down my life for her. You looking me in the eyes?"

Mikey nodded.

"I'm telling you, as God is my witness, she is going to be so covered…FBI agents up that guy's ass so far he won't be able to sit down for a week once we're through with him. Now you don't have to be comfortable with this. You don't have to like it. Hell, I don't like it at all. But we want to get your father back, and we want to nail the real murderer."

At four thirty, it was time for me to be wired up, get my bulletproof vest on and get ready. I asked to see Lewis alone. The two of us went into Joe's office.

"Now, Billie," he said, smiling mischievously. "I know you're about to declare your undying, unrequited love for me."

"Yeah, that's it."

"See…and I need to tell you that it's only because you're about to face a terrible danger that you're feeling this way."

"Lewis, shut up."

"But I love you, too. In fact, my last will and testament leaves my brain collection to you."

"I should have known that it was hopeless, that I couldn't have a serious conversation with you."

"Converse away, my sweet."

"I just…Lewis, how good an agent is this Two Trees?"

"The best. Even if he is afraid of a little hairy spider."

"I'm afraid. Not for me, but for my dad. I just don't want anything to happen to him. You know, when he was younger, I never feared for him. He was invincible, you know? But he's in his sixties now."

"Billie, if there's one person I am not worried about in this whole unmitigated disaster, it's your father. They turn their backs for one instant, and they'll find themselves dead. Now you go and nail them."

I nodded.

"And, Billie?"

"Hmm?"

"I really will leave you my brain collection."

I rolled my eyes and went out to say goodbye to everyone else. David kissed me and whispered, "See you and your father when you get back."

Mikey was riding with two agents. In fact,

agents filled the house. They had taken my cell phone and put both a GPS and bugging device in it. A GPS device was on my car. I was wired. I was wearing a bulletproof vest—which didn't show under my winter jacket, which bulked me up already. I had been instructed as well as possible on how to react to multiple scenarios. We got word from Greenwood Lake that my father was not with Jack.

"They'll have him stashed somewhere, Billie. Keep him talking. He may slip up," Tommy told me. He put the tiniest of earpieces in my ear—it was smaller than my pinky nail. As he put it in place, he told me, "Just so you know, you're never alone."

I was ready to leave, but C.C. stopped me. She handed me something.

"What's this?" I looked down at my palm.

"Scapulars."

"What?"

"You're Catholic, you should know," she teased.

"Please. I'm a Christmas-Easter Catholic. If that."

"You can wear them under your clothes and they're a form of protection. These have been blessed by Pope John Paul. I'd feel better if you wore them under your coat."

I couldn't say no to her, so I took them.

"Thanks, C.C."

I turned and left the house with Tommy and about ten agents. They all got into various unmarked cars, and I got into mine.

"You there, Billie?"

I heard Tommy's voice in my ear. My car, I knew, was now wired so they could hear anything that took place inside it. Jack knew how much the Quinns despised law enforcement, so hopefully he wouldn't suspect they were with me.

"I'm here."

"Good luck."

"Thanks."

I pulled out of Joe's driveway and made my way to Route 9W.

Jack, I thought, *did I ever really know you?*

"Scotch, please. Rocks."

Jack had come into Quinn's around ten. I had been tending bar, covering a few shifts while my cousin Shelley was out having her twin boys.

"Any particular brand? Johnnie Walker Red? Glenfiddich? Dewar's?"

"I'll take a Dewar's."

I poured him his scotch while sizing him up. I took him for a cop right away. It was a Quinn family trait to be able to spot them from a mile off. His hair was perfectly trimmed, his carriage just a shade stiff, his posture a little too perfect. And he moved his eyes from left to right, right to left, scanning the room, a habit of criminals—or cops.

"Haven't see you here before," I said.

"I come in every once in a while."

"I'm Billie."

"Jack."

"Nice to meet you."

I moved down the bar, busying myself with other customers. I refilled all the bowls of peanuts in the bar and went to the one near him to refill it.

"I'll have another." He slid his glass across the bar.

I poured him another one. Then I got busy again. Eventually, though, he was asking for his fifth scotch.

"You driving?"

"Yup."

"You know, I'd feel a lot better if you'd let me call you a cab. Quinn's will pay for it."

"Look, I'm a cop. Who's gonna arrest me for a DUI?"

"I don't care if you're the mayor, you're not getting into a car until you sober up. Let me make a pot of coffee."

"Don't bother."

"Look, you run over some kid, or kill a family in a car, and you won't forgive yourself—and neither will I."

At the mention of kids, a family, I watched his face change. One minute, he was hostile, a little sneering. The next, he was like a beaten dog with its tail between its legs.

"Okay. I'll take that coffee."

I nodded and went to brew a fresh pot for the bar area. When I came back, I poured him a piping hot cup.

"How do you take it?"

"Black."

"All right, then, bottoms up." I grinned at him.

He sipped his coffee. Eventually, the bar crowd thinned out. I kept pouring him hot coffee. He kept drinking it.

"You got any kids?" he asked me sometime after one in the morning.

"No. I'd like to someday. It's just I barely have time to date, let alone get married and have a baby. You?"

He nodded. "I did. She, um, got sick. You know, I still don't know what to say when people ask me. You know, 'Do you have kids?' I don't know whether to say yes or not."

I looked at him. I'd been tending bar at

Quinn's Pub, first for college money and then to help out for vacationing bartenders, for years. I always knew being a bartender was part psychology, part mixology. And frankly, in a place like Quinn's, most people order beer or something simple, like scotch, Jack Daniel's and Coke, or vodka drinks, so the mixology part was pretty basic.

I leaned over and put my elbows on the bar. "If it was me, I'd say yeah. I'm a dad. Because even if your little girl is in heaven, you'll always be her daddy."

I looked him in the eyes. I watched him swallow hard, his voice got gruff, hoarse, and he said, "Thanks."

I moved away from him, busying myself with putting things away now that the night was nearly done. He watched me. Out of the corner of my eye, I watched him.

I went back to him. "Another coffee for the road?"

He nodded. I poured. Then he asked me, "You know the Quinns?"

"The owners? Sure do."

"Hmm. I once busted one of the nephews of the big guy. He took a swing at me."

"Sounds like one of my cousins."

"Cousins?"

I nodded. Might as well get all our cards on the table. I was a Quinn. He was a grieving father.

"Billie *Quinn*. My dad is the 'big guy.'"

"Oh."

"I'm a criminalist. I work at the lab in Bloomsbury when I'm not subbing behind the bar. Assistant director and right-hand woman to the director. Know him? Lewis LeBarge?"

He shook his head.

"It bug you that I'm a cop?"

"It bug you that I'm Frank Quinn's daughter?"

"Nah. I've always been a cop on the edge."

Funny how you can look back on your life and see all the moments when trouble walked in your door, or when you should have taken a different path. What might have happened if I'd begged my mother not to leave? What might have happened if I had simply let the alcoholic cop take a cab and hadn't given him my number?

I drove on toward Greenwood Lake. The night was crystal clear and the farther north I got, the more stars I could see. The moon was about half-full, and it illuminated the tree line as the sun set. I was dressed warm in layer after layer. I had no idea what would happen on the island or how long I would be out in the cold night air. I wasn't relishing what was to come, at all.

I turned off the main road and found the boat landing Jack and I used to launch from. Sure enough, a big rowboat was waiting, oars resting in the bottom of it. I whispered aloud to the agents listening in, "Well boys, here we go. Tell my brother I love him."

Chapter 24

I looked at the lake. It was dark out now, and the lake was even darker. Frigid water lapped at my ankles, and a little bit of ice crusted at the edges of the lake. I had better be certain I didn't fall in at any point.

Fortunately, I wore my hiking boots, thick and waterproof. I pushed on the rowboat and hopped in, steadying myself. I put the oars in the oarlocks and started toward the middle of the lake, though I couldn't see the island as the moon slipped behind a cloud. A big lantern-style flashlight and a life vest were also in the boat, but I couldn't imagine adding more bulk to my frame with the life vest.

I shivered a bit as I rowed, the wind hitting my face and making my eyes tear involuntarily. "God, it's freezing," I said.

The lake was silent. I could hear the sound of the occasional car on the road, a sort of faraway whoosh, but mostly I heard the sound of my oars hitting the water, and then the mechanical sound of the oarlocks.

When I had rowed pretty far out, I stopped to get my bearings. The island was there in the distance. My muscles ached, but I thought of my father and got a burst of energy, steeling myself against the cold and dipping my oars in the lake again.

Finally, I reached the shoreline of the island. I rowed around in a circle to see where Jack had moored his boat. Around the back side of the lake was a giant fallen tree. His rowboat was there, tied with a rope to one of the branches and then dragged up to shore.

"Go on, tie it." I heard his voice, though I couldn't see him yet. "I'll help you."

I saw a rope coiled in the bow of the boat. I grabbed it and threw it over the tree trunk. I felt the boat being pulled as he tugged on the rope. Cautiously, when I felt the boat actually hit land, I made my way to the point at the front of the rowboat and hopped out, my boots crunching on ice.

"Where are you?" I called out.

"Here."

I whirled around, and there he was, looking thinner than I remembered, and tired.

"Hi, Jack. I'm here. Where's my dad?"

"Where's Cammie's underwear?"

I pulled the fake pair of panties out of my pocket and thrust them at him, sealed in the Ziploc bag. "I could lose my job over this."

"Lewis won't fire you." He shoved them in his jacket pocket.

"The film is in there, too."

"You have duplicates?"

"No. There wasn't time. Or a reason. I wasn't expecting my father to be kidnapped, Jack. I wasn't expecting any of this, least of all for there to be a personal connection to the suicide king murders."

"Would you believe me if I told you I had nothing to do with her murder?"

"I don't know," I said. I wanted to get him to trust me. "I guess it would depend on what you had to say."

"Come on," he said. "Over here. I have a little Coleman stove. We'll light it to keep you warm and I've got a thermos of hot coffee. I have a couple of blankets, too."

"What if someone on shore sees the fire?"

"It's small enough. Come on." Out of, I guess, instinct, he grabbed my hand. As if all this hadn't come to pass and we were still close. I pulled my hand away as soon as we got to the stove, which he had in the center of a fire ring made of gathered stones.

I sat down, and he passed me a thick wool blanket and lit the stove.

"Thanks," I muttered. "Jack…look, I want to know where my father is."

"I'll tell you. After you give me the chance to tell you the truth."

"Fine." I wrapped the blanket tighter around me and leaned a little closer to the stove's warmth.

"Want some coffee?"

"No. My stomach already hurts from what you've done. I couldn't drink coffee if I wanted to."

"I haven't had a drink in thirty-four days, Billie. Thirty-four days. Got a thirty-day coin from A.A. and everything."

I had attended a few Al-Anon meetings when we were dating. "Yeah? What are you going to do when it gets to the amends step? Where you have to admit all you've done wrong? You're just going to skip over that part?"

He hung his head for a second. "I still love you, Billie. I know right now you're really upset with me. But you know how I am when I'm drinking, I mess up."

"Yeah. You murder people."

"I didn't. Will you listen to me, please?"

"Fine."

"All right." He took a deep breath and let it out slowly. I could see the wisps of his breath swirl around him in the freezing temperature. "Cammie Whitaker was my lover. It was a screwed-up thing to do, but I sort of…my marriage was a mess. We'd been trying to have a baby, and…we weren't successful. Carol, God…she never talked about anything else. Baby, baby, baby. It was like we had nothing else in our lives but to watch when she ovulated. We were at each other's throats. And I had just gotten my promotion. Like a lot of guys on the job, ambitious guys, I felt like I had to make my mark. I was putting in so many hours, I was falling asleep in my car. Meantime, we're broke from seeing fertility specialists. Anyway, one night, I'm onto a possible drug bust. Marty and I, we end up finding a gym bag full of cash. Untraceable. Dealer was shot dead in his place before we arrived. So we pocketed the cash."

"What?"

"Billie, you know what it's like to have trouble paying your electric bill while the bad guys live like kings and drive fancy cars you couldn't afford if you saved for ten years? I did it and I'm ashamed of it—but part of me isn't. And Marty talks me into investing with him in a club."

"A strip club."

He nodded. "It didn't feel right, but I was drinking a bit too much at the time. And investing in the club? It made me drink more. I didn't even tell my wife about it. I just put away the cash saving for a house. Anyway, I used to go to this one bar after work where Cammie was the bartender. She was a kid. A real kid. But she was a good listener. Sweet. And before I knew it, I thought I was in love with her."

"Were you?" I managed to croak, though my throat had gone completely dry.

"I think so. But then my wife got pregnant. I mean, we had waited so long for a baby. And then out of nowhere, she's pregnant. So I broke it off with Cammie."

"And what happened when you did?"

"She took it bad. She was a mess. I was, too,

but I just felt like it would be wrong not to try to make it work with Carol. I buried myself in my job—*the* job. And I was spending time at the club. Making some decent money out of it. And then Cammie showed up."

"At the club?"

"Yeah. She got Rick to give her a job—Marty had pulled together the deal with the four of us. I was really, really upset. She had no business doing that kind of work. She had no business there. Then Rick talked her into taking some side work. By now I was in so deep I felt like I couldn't get out, Billie. And I was sick about Cammie. Sick. She was trying to make me mad, make me rescue her. I think she had a…complex about that. Wanting to be rescued. Knight in shining armor."

"Why didn't you just fire her? I mean, these guys were your friends, right?"

"Yes and no. Friends, but a lot of locker room crap. We were hard on each other. Always this edge to it. Rick said she could quit but he wouldn't fire her. She was bringing in too much money."

I shook my head slowly, back and forth. "Poor thing."

"Yeah," he whispered. "So then I reached a point, I had to see her outside of that place, outside of the club. So I went to her apartment. God, just seeing her, I felt the way I always had. We made love. I told her I wanted her to stop that shit. But then she pressured me. Was I going to leave my wife, all that. I told her about the baby, and she went completely insane, so I left. I drove around and around and around. Thinking. Came back…and now this guy's there. Falco. So I mean, I went back to make things right. I figure, yes, my wife is having a baby, but we're not in love. Maybe I can somehow, after the baby comes, leave my wife. There was more money now, and I thought maybe I could somehow do it. But Falco is there."

"And Cammie was nasty to you."

"Yeah. She was playing me. Not like I blame her. I leave…and next thing I know, she turns up dead. I had used a condom. Thought I was safe. I kept my mouth shut. I figured it was Falco. Fuck it. Let him rot in there and throw away the key."

"What about the card? The playing card?"

"I didn't leave it. I assumed he had."

I wanted to throw up. I mean, aside from the fact that I was upset over Jack's moral and personal failures, if Jack was telling the truth, it opened up the tiniest window that David was guilty. Who was the real sociopath?

"But his DNA wasn't inside Cammie, Jack. Yours was."

"Right. But I didn't kill her. Now, I may go to prison for obstructing justice, for some other bullshit, now that you and your pals stuck your noses in here, but I ain't going in for murder. I didn't kill her."

"So you're saying Falco did it?"

"I assumed so. Until later, a few years later, I find out that Rick did it."

"Why?"

"She was playing everybody. She was so messed up, she was sleeping with him to get back at me, and she was doing drugs. He cut her off. Wasn't going to risk a moneymaker. And then she started making a lot of noise about going to the feds, the IRS and the goddamn chief of police about our little club and what was going on there."

"So he killed her?"

"Yeah. He went to her with drugs, said he was sorry. She could have all the drugs she wanted. But he slipped her something else. Something to paralyze her. And then he killed her. Turns out a few girls wanted out. He did it as a warning. You don't fuck with the suicide king."

"You have to go to the police, Jack."

"We *are* the police."

"Well, you need to make things right. You left a man to rot in prison knowing all this. And what about this girl in Atlantic City?"

"We all made a pact to keep our mouths shut. We felt like Rick was the loose cannon, so we kept a tight rein on him. As we expanded, we each sort of ran our own operation. That girl in Atlantic City, she was turning tricks on the side and apparently had stolen our little black book, made copies. That book has got celebrities in it, politicians. She was blackmailing us. By then Falco was out, and we couldn't risk attention falling on us. This time, Marty killed her and he did it so…well, like a copycat, like Falco was still guilty. Didn't count on you falling in love with the guy, Billie. Didn't count on DNA clearing him."

"Jack, you're an accessory to murder. You think having those panties is going to keep you out of jail? You think you telling me all this is going to sway me?"

"Without my DNA, there's nothing to tie me to her."

"Except your three partners—sooner or later, when the D.A. lays it all out, they'll roll on you. You're all going to go to prison, Jack."

"He who makes the best deal, wins. Just like

in poker. Without the DNA, I have the better hand, the better story. I know the truth."

"Jack…this isn't a poker game. It's a crime." I stood up. "I want to know where my father is."

"Do you love this guy, Falco?" He looked up at me, his face anxious.

"Jack…" He looked so sad. "Whatever we had is over. It was over before I met him. It was over when you couldn't stop drinking."

"But I've stopped now."

"I know. But you've been hiding so many secrets. You're a dirty cop, Jack."

"I'm out of it. I swear. Billie…look, you know when I lost Katie, I was a wreck. I've fucked up in my life, but I'm looking to straighten out now. And in all my life, Billie, you're the one I loved. I swear it. You know how we are."

"We're combustible, Jack. There was always something intense between us, but that can't be anymore. I'm going back to shore right now, and I want you to tell me where my dad is."

"I'll take you to him."

"You swear?"

"I swear. Come on."

He extinguished the stove, and gathered the blankets. We made our way back to the rowboats. Dry leaves swirled in the wind.

"We'll go in this boat," he said. "Leave the other one. I'll row. Climb in."

I stepped into the rowboat, and he pushed us off, then jumped in himself. He went in the middle seat, with me in the bow, and started rowing.

"Did you ever love me, Billie?"

I nodded. "I loved who I thought you were."

We rowed under the starry sky. Suddenly, Jack stopped.

"What was that?"

"What?" I asked warily.

"That flash on the shore. I saw a light flash."

"So?"

"So, I don't like it. You tell anyone you were coming here?"

"My brother. That's it. And you know Mikey. It's not like he's going to go to the cops. He hates cops. And now, frankly, after hearing your story, I do, too."

"Are you wired?"

"What?"

"I don't like this." He pulled the panties and film out of his jacket pocket and out of their plastic bag. He plunged them into the water, using his oar to sink the underwear.

"Jack…"

"Shut up." He pulled out a gun.

"Jack, don't…we don't need guns between us."

A couple of minutes later, two helicopters swooped across the night sky, shining lights on us. On the shore, cop cars lit up their headlights, and someone was on a bullhorn, telling him to put down his weapon. Jack grabbed me and pulled me to my feet. Both of us were standing in the boat, which was unsteady. He held the gun to my head.

"Whoa, Jack…don't do this."

"You lied to me, Billie."

"I lied to you? You kidnapped my father, Jack!"

"PUT THE GUN DOWN!" A male voice spoke authoritatively over the bullhorn.

"If I go down, Billie, you're going with me. Tell them to back off."

"Guys…" I said. "Things are getting hairy here. Please back off."

The helicopters shone bright lights on our boat, and the gusts from their propellers stirred up the water, which shook the boat.

"Back off!" Jack screamed. One of the helicopters dipped a little, and we started losing our balance. I put my hands out to grab the sides of the boat, but we both fell into the water.

At the first touch of the water, I felt a shock

go through me like the snap of electricity, then a wall of pain. I opened my eyes underwater, but could see nothing. I looked up and could see the light of the helicopter, and I tried to move toward it but found my arms were like lead. I gulped in cold water, which seared my lungs. Already, my brain couldn't think. I felt as though I was moving in slow motion.

Jack grabbed me and pulled me to the surface. I gasped for air and shrieked.

"Pull off some of your clothes."

"I c-c-c-an't." My teeth chattered so much I felt as if I was actually breaking my molars.

I was weighted down with the bulletproof vest, with my heavy boots and winter clothes.

Jack grabbed me, and we were face-to-face, both shivering.

"I'm not going to prison," he said, holding on to me. My brain hurt, my temples throbbed.

"Jack…we need to…get…back in the boat."

I tried to stretch an arm toward it, but I couldn't.

From the helicopter, someone dropped a life ring. It fell to the water a few feet from me.

I looked at Jack. His face was white, completely pale. I assumed I looked the same. Everything hurt, and I felt us both sinking a bit.

"Jack," I whispered desperately.

"I'm going to Katie," he said.

"Don't. Don't." I tried to crane my neck. Three men looked poised to dive into the lake. Motorboats were coming toward us.

"Let her go," someone shouted.

Jack stared at me, his eyes resolute.

"Where's Daddy? Don't do this to me. You…know what I've…gone through…my mom."

"Stone table," he said, then slipped under the surface of the water.

I felt myself sinking with him, his arms still wrapped around me. He was giving up, intentionally allowing the water to carry us to the depths. I tried to kick my feet, but found I couldn't. I took my hands and pried his fingers from me. He sank down farther until I couldn't see him. I tried to move toward the surface, but couldn't reach it.

Miraculously, I felt someone pulling me up. Pulling me up toward the light. Then, the world went black.

Chapter 25

I woke up in an ambulance, wrapped in tons of blankets. I was also, I thought, naked.

"Yes. I got to see your ass."

The voice was Lewis's. I turned my head. "What?"

"They took your wet clothes off and I got to see you naked. I could spend the rest of my life happily living off that specific memory."

"Fuck off," I said.

He leaned down over the stretcher and kissed the top of my wet head. "If anything had happened to you, I'd never have gotten over it. I'll send your brother in."

Lewis got out of the ambulance and Mikey came in. "Hey…little sis. How are you?"

"Cold."

"They got these warmers on you. Gonna take you to the hospital."

"Not until we find Daddy."

"We heard what he said, over the wire, but Jack was out of his mind with hypothermia, honey. We don't know where Dad is. The FBI have raided all the clubs, but basically, seems like Jack took Dad on his own. He wanted insurance that he wouldn't get the rap for the murder."

"No." I tried to sit up and felt as though my muscles had turned to spaghetti. I had never ached so much in my entire life.

"Baby…they're in Jack's apartment now. They're trying to find Daddy." Mikey put his lips on my forehead. "Man, your skin is like icicles."

"Get me out of here. Get me something to wear."

"No…Billie, baby, come on. I can't tell you how scared I was for you."

"Jack knew I lost Mom. He lost Katie. He wouldn't do that. He wouldn't let Daddy die. He told me someplace real. Stone table. Is that a bar, a restaurant? He's somewhere, Mikey."

I groaned and sat up. "I'm not going to the hospital, so you might as well find me clothes."

"Shit. Someone's gotta talk some sense into that stubborn Quinn head of yours."

He ducked out of the ambulance, but he returned a couple of minutes later with an FBI jacket and a pair of sweats.

"Sweats are from Lewis. Were in his trunk. Jacket's from an agent. Got a pair of socks here from Lewis's workout bag, too. Don't know if they're *clean.*"

"You think I care? Give them to me."

Still shaking, I tried to dress myself but found my fingers didn't listen to my brain. "What's up with my hands?"

"You were in a freezing lake for five minutes loaded down with a vest and everything else. You're lucky you didn't drown like Jack."

"Help me," I pleaded with Mikey. He came over to me and buttoned my jacket.

"Stand up. Put your hands on my shoulder."

He's my brother, so I didn't feel embarrassed. He got me dressed, then pulled all the blankets from the stretcher around me. He opened the doors to the ambulance and motioned for Tommy Two Trees to come over.

"She ain't listening to me, buddy."

Tommy took one look at me and started saying, "Oh, no…oh, no…you get back on that stretcher."

I shook my head. "Not until we find my dad. So you either help me or I'm walking away with my brother. And if I die or get sick or whatever, it's on your conscience."

"Listen, I'll just arrest you, Billie. Doesn't matter to me how I keep you safe and get you medical help."

"Fine. I'll go to the media with *that*."

He sighed. "Look, we're going to find your dad."

"Punch in stone table on a search engine."

"Did. Nothing. No bar, no restaurant for a five-hundred-mile radius with that name."

My eyes hurt. My eyelashes hurt. Everything hurt, but I tried to focus. I felt as if I had a migraine.

"Wait!"

"What?" Tommy asked.

"Jack…Jack knew this island because he hunted and fished. That was why it was our place. Shit…wait. Put in 'stone table' and all the various state parks around here. I have a hunch."

Tommy nodded and disappeared. I huddled next to the heat.

Ten minutes later, Tommy came back.

"We have a match. A stone formation at the top of a mountain. That fucker might have been telling the truth after all. We're taking the helicopters."

"We're coming," I said.

"Now, listen, you two, I don't know what we're going to find and you're supposed to be on your way to the hospital, not going up in a copter on a wild-goose chase."

"It's not going to be a wild-goose chase. I know Jack was telling me the truth. Please, Tommy."

Tommy spun around and cursed into the wind, then turned back. "All right, damn. Damn, damn, damn. You can come. But you're staying in the helicopter."

He spoke into a gadget of some sort. We were in a parking lot, with FBI cars, cop cars and flashing lights. Two copters appeared in the sky and landed in the lot.

I looked at Mikey. "My legs aren't working and I don't have shoes. Can you carry me?"

Mikey nodded and scooped me up. The two of us and Two Trees darted across the parking lot. Lewis came up to us.

"She needs to go to the hospital!"

"Look, Lewis," Tommy said. "This is easier than dealing with her."

"Let's go, guys," I urged.

We left Lewis and maneuvered over to the

helicopters, their blades whirring. Mikey ducked, carrying me, and whispered in my ear, "Whatever happens, I got your back."

I nodded. He settled me into a corner of the helicopter. Tommy climbed on, along with a few extra agents, and then we took off, my stomach feeling as though it lifted and then sank. I was nauseous.

Mikey kept an arm around me, and I continued to shiver. The two copters flew through the night. I looked out the window into the darkness wondering what we would find at the stone table.

"How cold is it out?" I asked.

Tommy looked out the window, too, not looking me in the eyes.

"With the wind chill it's twenty below."

"Figures he picks some of the coldest weather all winter for this shit." I fought back tears. I thought of Jack's pale face disappearing into the depths of the lake.

"Dad's a fighter," Mikey said.

I nodded. But I also knew my father was a city guy—his idea of taking us camping was heading down to Atlantic City for the weekend and letting us play in the sand while he hit the casinos. He wasn't a fisherman or a hunter. I didn't even know if he owned warm enough clothes for a night as cold as tonight.

We hovered over the top of the mountain.

"Where are we going to land?" I asked Tommy.

"We're not. Agents are going to rappel down. It's our only choice."

"Let me go," I begged.

"Not a chance. For one thing, you're not strong enough right now. Let the agents go."

I watched as FBI agents opened the helicopter door and prepared to climb out and down ropes. I was terrified. All I could do was hope that Mikey and I wouldn't lose our only parent to a murderer—we'd been the victim of one killer before, and I couldn't bear the thought of our family being victim to a second one.

Lights beamed down on the mountaintop. I looked out the helicopter window as agents swarmed the stone formation. It did look like a table. One rock leaned on another. It was smooth, like a tabletop. Agents scurried, dressed in black, reminding me of ants invading a picnic.

Tommy came over to me. "I'm going down. Seems to me a friend should be there to find your father. Okay if I leave the two of you alone in here with the pilots?"

We nodded.

I watched as Tommy, dressed in black pants

and a jacket with FBI emblazoned on the back, disappeared out the helicopter.

Mikey held me close and talked to me over the noise of whirring helicopter blades.

"Whatever happens, me and you are going to be okay, Billie."

I nodded. "I'm sorry, Mikey."

"Why? What do you have to be sorry for?"

"For one thing, I was involved with Jack."

"He fooled us all. Billie, he was on the edge, but we all thought it was the booze. Not this shit."

"And the Justice Foundation. If Lewis and I hadn't gotten involved, none of this would have happened."

I squeezed my eyes shut, willing away tears.

"Hey…you're the smart one in the family. I'm proud of you."

He tousled my hair, and we sat in the helicopter and waited. I prayed. I could hear Mikey saying "please, please, please" under his breath.

I could hear someone talking to the pilot over the radio. The copilot looked back and said, "We got him. He's alive."

I hugged my brother as hard as I could. "You hear that?"

"See? The Quinns are tough, baby. The Quinns are tough."

"Would be nice if we didn't have to be."

"Come on…it's who we are."

I thought about being in that lake with Jack. I thought about *why* I was there. To do the right thing. Because I could. Because even though I had fears, I believed in something bigger than myself. I was a Quinn. I was tough. It was who I was.

Chapter 26

In my hospital bed, dehydrated, being treated for exposure and some frostbite, I thought of my mother. And as I looked at all the flowers that filled my room, I had a long-forgotten memory of her.

She used to have a garden in our backyard. Every spring, she would go out to the beds and mulch and turn the earth. I remember watching her in the crisp spring air. She'd tuck a stray hair behind her ear, and breathe in deep.

"Smell the spring, Billie, can you smell it?"

I nodded, but I wasn't sure I really could. I watched as she planted flowers into holes she dug with her hand trowel. Gladiolas and tulips.

When it got a little warmer, she would plant Shasta daisies, sunflowers, pansies and peonies, and our kitchen would be transformed into a miniature nursery. Tomato plants and green pepper plants, cucumber plants and little lettuce plants would be nurtured in tiny little pots and starter kits, waiting to be transplanted out in the big garden. All summer, then, we'd have fresh vegetables.

After my mother was murdered, we never planted the garden again. My father didn't know a thing about plants, and Mikey and I were too young. But even today, when I visit Dad in springtime, old plants, gone wild over time, still push up out of the beds. They're straggly and untidy; they wouldn't win a ribbon at a flower show, but they were part of her.

I climbed out of my bed and pulled on my robe over the arm that didn't have an IV in it. Twenty-four hours later and I was just starting to feel warm, really warm, inside. I still felt stiff and achy, but I was looking forward to going home.

I walked over to the windowsill, dragging

my IV pole. All the floral arrangements sat in the window, filling the room with a beautiful aroma. Joe, of course, king of the grand gesture, had sent an enormous arrangement that had to have cost a couple of hundred dollars. Large lilies and roses and delicate lilies of the valley spilled out of a crystal vase. I read the card:

TO JUSTICE...
AND TRUE FRIENDS, JOE

Lewis, in his usual sick-humor way, sent me a funeral arrangement. A standing arrangement like the ones mourners would see in a funeral home stood in one corner. I shook my head and read the card:

YOU SCARED ME THERE, QUINN.
LOVE, LEWIS AND RIPPER

Mikey had sent me a dozen red roses. Tommy Two Trees sent me a basket of wildflowers, with a card that read:

YOU WOULD HAVE MADE A HELL OF AN AGENT, BUT MY GUESS IS KEEPING UP WITH LEWIS IS TWICE AS DANGEROUS, T-CUBED

And David had sent an arrangement. It was small, delicate, a single orchid. His card was simply signed:

LOVE, DAVID.

I slid my feet into my slippers and opened the door and poked my head out. I didn't see any nurses—they wanted me to stay in bed—and so I slipped across the hall.

Daddy was sleeping.

They had found him in a cave, tied up. His lamp had gone through its batteries, and he'd been left with no food or water. Jack had marched him up that mountain during the day, at gunpoint. If Jack hadn't told me "stone table," my father would have died, something that still made my insides queasy.

He had suffered in the cave. Frostbite, hypothermia, and his heart rate got very erratic.

Sleeping, my dad looked peaceful. He had gotten older, sort of without my realizing it, in the same way I think it still stunned him that I nearly had my doctorate and I lived my own life.

I sat on the edge of his bed, and brushed my hand across his forehead. His eyelids fluttered.

"Billie." He smiled at me.

"Hey, Daddy." I smiled back at him.

"You saved my life, you know."

"Not really. It was me who got you in that mess to begin with."

"But you went out onto that lake. You got Jack to tell you where I was."

I shrugged. "I was so scared, Dad."

He didn't say anything, just grabbed my hand. "You know, Billie, I didn't think I'd ever see you again. When the batteries started going on the lantern, and then it got pitch-black, I started talking to your mother."

I swallowed hard.

"I haven't been a saint. You know that. Your brother and I...we're one sort of person. And you...you're a different sort. And I told your mother that I wouldn't have wanted to die without you knowing I'm proud of you. This wasn't your fault. You got an innocent man out of prison. And...I wouldn't want you to stop because of what happened."

"I don't know, Dad."

In truth, as I lay in my hospital bed, I had wondered what to do. Did I have the stomach to keep doing work for the Justice Foundation? Was it in me?

"You do know."

I nodded.

"And one of these days, I really think you're going to solve your mother's murder. And then she can rest in peace. Real peace."

"I love you, Daddy."

"Love you, too."

I hugged him and then went back across the hallway to my room. Lewis was waiting.

"What about staying in bed do you not understand, Billie?"

"I was just visiting my dad. Thanks for the flower arrangement, by the way. I can't tell you the looks I've received from the nurses."

"Don't mention it."

I climbed back into bed and snuggled down under the four blankets they had on my bed.

"I can't get the picture of Jack in that lake out of my mind."

"It's better he go to wherever it is we all go than face prison as a cop."

"You know, that sounded faintly agnostic, or even a touch spiritual, instead of your usual atheist viewpoint. C.C. is rubbing off on you."

"Billie, she's gone."

"What do you mean, she's gone?"

"She asked me to give you this." He handed me a letter.

"What do you mean, she's gone?" I asked again.

"She's left for a spiritual retreat. She has some soul-searching to do. Open the letter."

I opened the envelope and unfolded the letter inside. It was written in a delicate script.

Dear Billie,

I need to do some spiritual seeking. I've gone to a place where I can pray and meditate and walk in silence, reflect on what I feel I need to do.

Watch over my beloved Lewis for me? I know you will. You two are lucky to have each other.

Also…I'm hoping you might visit a couple of prisoners for me. They're men whose cases the Foundation is taking on, and they need to know they will not be forgotten, that someone cares. You can do that for me, right? Joe has their names and case files.

Thank you, Billie. I feel like our work is bigger, with the four of us, than any one of us could do alone. Fate has brought us together.

Your friend,
C.C.

I looked up at Lewis. "She wants me to visit prisoners."

"I know," he said.

"Lewis…do you think we should go on with this stuff?"

He nodded. "She's right. It's bigger than all of us. It's a calling of its own sort."

"You okay? I mean, with her going away?"

"Just gives me another reason to be my usual melancholy self."

"This was hard, Lewis."

"Yeah…but you're a Quinn. You know they're planning a big party when you and your father get out of here."

"We Quinns don't need much of a reason for a party. Did I tell you about the time we had one because my uncle beat a speeding ticket?"

He smiled. "Didn't this whole adventure start with a Quinn party?"

"Yeah. And a bar fight."

"Well, it wouldn't be a Quinn party without one."

My father and I were released a day apart from each other, and that weekend we had a blowout bash to celebrate.

Tommy Two Trees came up to me in the

midst of the chaos. "Your father just took me for forty bucks at the pool table."

"He's milking all that sympathy."

"Lewis tells me you two are sticking with the Foundation."

I nodded, looking across the room at David as he sat with Mikey, laughing and playing cards. He'd still be in prison if it weren't for C.C. and Joe taking his case.

"Do me a favor then, keep my card handy. Something tells me you and Lewis are a magnet for trouble. Never know when you'll need me."

"Thanks. For everything, Tommy."

He clasped his hands together and bowed. "You're quite a warrior."

I bowed back.

Then I walked across the room to David. He leaned back a bit and I sat on his lap and planted a kiss on his cheek.

"Hey, beautiful," he breathed in my ear, sending a shiver through me. He slid one hand across my back and then laid down four jacks.

"Four of a kind, gentlemen. I believe the pot is mine."

"Shit!" Mikey said and threw his cards down. "Let me go get more beer. At least if I'm going to lose, I'm going to get good and drunk doing it."

I laughed. Suddenly, I heard a commotion by the door. I rolled my eyes. "The Murphy brothers just arrived."

Next thing I knew, chairs were flying. David and I ducked under the table. He grabbed my face and kissed me.

"I'd like to tell you never to scare me again like you did, Billie, but somehow I don't think that's possible."

I looked at him. "I'm still going to work with Joe and C.C."

"I know."

"And someday I'm going to solve my mother's murder."

"I believe you."

I peered out from under the table. The Quinns were winning. "And now I'm going to go break up this fight."

I crawled out from under the table, just as I saw Lewis get hit by a good right hook from one of the Murphys.

Just another Friday night.

Chapter 1

The bus the terrorists had demanded was just pulling up in front of the Olympic Village apartment building. The casual observer wouldn't see the dozen German Army snipers lying in wait around the street, but Isabella Torres was no casual observer. A trained spotter for military snipers, she picked out the vital details.

An Olympic flag hung limp behind the policeman on the roof, which meant good wind conditions for the shooters. A shadow fell on the floor inside the front door—one of the terrorists, no doubt there in preparation for the transfer of the eleven surviving Israeli hostages. The bus driver's bulging muscles and lack of visible fear marked him as German Special Forces.

A flurry of German radio chatter announced the eight Palestinian Arabs were approaching the exit with their hostages. Given that there were more prisoners than guards, they'd have to move the hostages as a group, surrounded by captors. That meant there's be an excellent opportunity for the snipers to get clear shots at the terrorists and end this thing here and now.

Each sniper had been assigned a single terrorist target. They'd been watching this nightmare unfold for nearly twenty-four hours through their telescopic gun sights. Long enough for the snipers to easily differentiate the terrorists, even though the Palestinians were dressed in identical track suits and wore black ski masks over their faces. It wasn't hard, really. Individual postures, movements and gestures were easy to pick out for a trained sharpshooter.

These would be very short-range shots. No more than a couple hundred meters. Kid stuff for snipers. They could put a bullet through Lincoln's eye on a penny at that range.

A command was barked across the sniper

radio net. It was clearly the order to prepare for their respective shots. Abrupt tension encompassed the scene. This was it. This crisis would be resolved in the next few seconds.

Two men in black ski masks appeared in the building's doorway. Isabella registered myriad details about them in the blink of an eye. Lean. Tense. Safeties off their AK-47s, fingers on the triggers. Weapons pointed outward at the police. Dumb. The guns ought to be pointed inward at the hostages so that even if the terrorists were shot, their reflexive grasps on the weapons would fire the guns into the tight cluster of Israeli athletes. The German authorities might not call the kill if the Palestinian guns were pointed at the hostages. But arrayed like this— the op was a go.

The terrorists and the Israelis shuffled forward in a tight phalanx. The athletes looked in equal parts terrified and defiant. The Palestinians were smart enough to make at least some effort to use the hostages as human shields. But it was no good. The shooters surrounding that bus all had their shots. There. The entire group of terrorists was exposed. Every one of them was in position for the snipers to take clear shots.

"Fire!" The command rang sharply across the sniper net in German.

Nothing happened.

Nothing happened!

"Fire, goddammit!" the German shouted into the radio.

Still nothing. Not a single one of the shooters took his shot.

Jack Scatalone, the Delta force colonel responsible for Isabella's training, held up a remote control and hit the pause button. He stepped in front of the frozen video image of the Israelis being herded into that bus. It shone obscenely across his crisp uniform, which was encrusted with row after row of medals for heroism. For successfully resolving this very sort of crisis without the complete breakdown of response they'd just witnessed.

Isabella—considered to be the top real-time visual intelligence analyst in the U.S. Air Force—still stared, her eyes opened wide in shock. She glanced at her teammates, the other five women who comprised the Medusas, the highly classified and first all-female Special Forces team in the U.S. military. They gaped, as well.

Isabella looked back at Jack and demanded, "You mean to tell me the Germans had the shots, were green-lighted to take them—hell, were ordered to take them—and they didn't?"

Jack's jaw rippled. "Kat? Care to explain?"

The Medusa's sniper, Katrina Kim, a petite woman of Asian descent, leaned forward. In a voice so calm it had to be masking fury at what they'd just witnessed, Kat said, "It's called the Munich Massacre Syndrome. The snipers spent so long watching the terrorists that they started to see them as human beings. As people. As scared young men. Not as targets. By the time they were ordered to shoot the terrorists, not a single one of the snipers could bring himself to pull the trigger."

Outrage still vibrated through Isabella's gut. "In all the news coverage I've seen of the '72 Olympics, nobody ever mentioned that the Germans had a chance to take out the terrorists and save those Israeli athletes." She glanced at the picture sprawled across Jack's chest. "Jeez, that was more than a chance. That was a slam dunk. The Palestinians handed themselves to the Germans on a silver platter."

"Conclusions?" Jack asked her.

The words, as dry as sawdust in her throat, wanted to stick, but she forced them out painfully. "The Munich Massacre never should have happened."

Jack nodded grimly. "That's correct. And out of this incident came the birth of counterterrorism as a specialty within the armed forces of most of the world's major armies. It completely changed how snipers are trained and deployed, and the psychological selection criteria for snipers were heavily revised, as well."

Isabella was still reeling. It could have been prevented. A tragic and vicious attack on a group of athletes who'd gone to Munich to celebrate the unity of mankind, to join with athletes from all over the world in a demonstration of the best of the human spirit. Instead, thirteen young men had been murdered in cold blood on the orders of Yasser Arafat. Worse, they could have been saved. It had been the ultimate corruption of everything the Olympics stood for.

"Why was this covered up?" she demanded.

Jack shrugged. "I can't speak for the politicians. It would've been pretty ugly for Germany to admit that Jews were slaughtered on their watch again. The whole idea behind taking the Olympics to Munich in the first place was for Germany to demonstrate that World War II was in the past."

Isabella stared at the frozen images of the terrorists looming on the screen over Jack's shoulder like vengeful ghosts. A cold finger of dread rippled down her spine. "And why did you choose today to teach us about this syndrome?"

Jack nodded tersely at her. "Very perceptive. I have a job for you ladies." He clicked the remote and the silver screen went blank behind him. "It's at the Olympics. And it involves a girl. Her name is Anya Khalid."

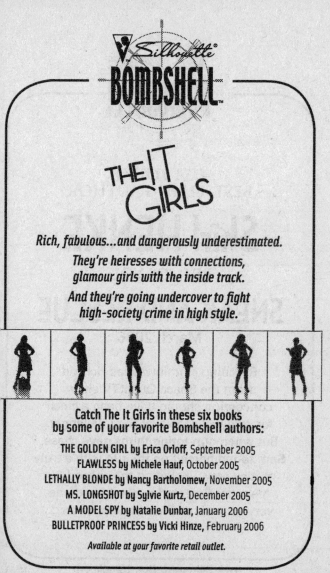

THE IT GIRLS

Rich, fabulous...and dangerously underestimated.

*They're heiresses with connections,
glamour girls with the inside track.*

*And they're going undercover to fight
high-society crime in high style.*

**Catch The It Girls in these six books
by some of your favorite Bombshell authors:**

THE GOLDEN GIRL by Erica Orloff, September 2005

FLAWLESS by Michele Hauf, October 2005

LETHALLY BLONDE by Nancy Bartholomew, November 2005

MS. LONGSHOT by Sylvie Kurtz, December 2005

A MODEL SPY by Natalie Dunbar, January 2006

BULLETPROOF PRINCESS by Vicki Hinze, February 2006

Available at your favorite retail outlet.

USA TODAY
BESTSELLING AUTHOR

Shirl HENKE

BRINGS YOU

SNEAK AND RESCUE
March 2006

Rescuing a brainwashed rich kid
from the Space Quest TV show
convention should have been a cinch
for retrieval specialist Sam Ballanger.
But when gun-toting thugs gave chase,
Sam found herself on the run with a truly
motley crew, including the spaced-out
teen, her flustered husband and one
very suspicious Elvis impersonator....

SBSAR

If you enjoyed what you just read,
then we've got an offer you can't resist!

Take 2 bestselling love stories FREE!
Plus get a FREE surprise gift!

Clip this page and mail it to Silhouette Reader Service®

IN U.S.A.	IN CANADA
3010 Walden Ave.	P.O. Box 609
P.O. Box 1867	Fort Erie, Ontario
Buffalo, N.Y. 14240-1867	L2A 5X3

YES! Please send me 2 free Silhouette Bombshell™ novels and my free surprise gift. After receiving them, if I don't wish to receive any more, I can return the shipping statement marked cancel. If I don't cancel, I will receive 4 brand-new novels every month, before they're available in stores! In the U.S.A., bill me at the bargain price of $4.69 plus 25¢ shipping & handling per book and applicable sales tax, if any*. In Canada, bill me at the bargain price of $5.24 plus 25¢ shipping & handling per book and applicable taxes**. That's the complete price and a savings of 10% off the cover prices—what a great deal! I understand that accepting the 2 free books and gift places me under no obligation ever to buy any books. I can always return a shipment and cancel at any time. Even if I never buy another book from Silhouettte, the 2 free books and gift are mine to keep forever.

200 HDN D34H
300 HDN D34J

Name _____ (PLEASE PRINT)

Address _____ Apt.#

City _____ State/Prov. _____ Zip/Postal Code

Not valid to current Silhouette Bombshell™ subscribers.

Want to try another series?
Call 1-800-873-8635 or visit www.morefreebooks.com.

* Terms and prices subject to change without notice. Sales tax applicable in N.Y.
** Canadian residents will be charged applicable provincial taxes and GST.
All orders subject to approval. Offer limited to one per household.
® and ™ are registered trademarks owned and used by the trademark owner and or its licensee.

BOMB04   ©2004 Harlequin Enterprises Limited

Where can a woman who has spent her life obliging others truly take time to rediscover herself? In the Coconut Zone...

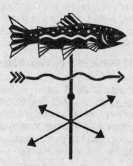

Off the Map

DORIEN KELLY

Available February 2006
TheNextNovel.com

BOMBSHELL

COMING NEXT MONTH

#77 SOMETHING WICKED by Evelyn Vaughn
The Grail Keepers

Kate Trillo never had a burning desire to follow the family tradition of goddess worship and witchcraft. But walking in on her sister's murder changed all of that. When Kate's curse on the perpetrator went dangerously awry and hit his twin brother, she was forced to search Greece, Turkey and Italy for the family grail that would reverse the damage. Would she find her way back from the dark side...before she lost her way forever?

#78 BULLETPROOF PRINCESS by Vicki Hinze
The It Girls

For modern-day princess Chloe St. John, working undercover for the Gotham Rose spies provided a perfect chance to prove herself in the face of her mother's constant criticism. But nothing in Chloe's royal playbook prepared her to take down a criminal mastermind who anticipated her every move...and a fellow Rose who might be ratting her out to the enemy.

#79 THE MEDUSA GAME by Cindy Dees
The Medusa Project

As part of the all-female Medusa Special Forces team, photo intelligence analyst Isabella Torres was ready for anything. The latest assignment to protect an Olympic figure skater receiving death threats seemed routine—until the Medusas uncovered a larger terrorist plot to put the winter games on ice. Now with thousands of lives at stake, and seeming ski bum Gunnar Holt as partner in security liaison, could Isabella keep her cool?

#80 RADICAL CURE by Olivia Gates

Field surgeon Calista St. James thought she'd put her latest deadly rescue mission behind her—until a violent, mysterious illness started laying her colleagues low. Tracking the problem to a rogue lab in Colombia on a tip from her vigilante father, Calista *knew* she could beat the clock and find a cure...provided she could get her difficult boss Damian De Luna to play by her rules, and keep her feelings for him in check....

SBCNM0106